Alan Hunter was born in Hoveton, Norfolk in 1922. He left school at the age of fourteen to work on his father's farm, spending his spare time sailing on the Norfolk Broads and writing nature notes for the *Eastern Evening News*. He also wrote poetry, some of which was published while he was in the RAF during the Second World War. By 1950, he was running his own bookshop in Norwich. In 1955, the first of what would become a series of forty-six George Gently novels was published. He died in 2005, aged eighty-two.

The Inspector George Gently series

Gently French

Alan Hunter

Constable & Robinson Ltd
55–56 Russell Square
London WC1B 4HP
www.constablerobinson.com

First published in the UK by Cassell & Company Ltd., 1973

This paperback edition published by C&R Crime,
an imprint of Constable & Robinson Ltd., 2013

A copy of the British Library Cataloguing in Publication
Data is available from the British Library.

ISBN 978-1-47210-870-8 (paperback)
ISBN 978-1-47210-878-4 (ebook)

Typeset by TW Typesetting, Plymouth, Devon

Printed and bound by CPI Group (UK) Ltd, Croydon, CR0 4YY

1 3 5 7 9 10 8 6 4 2

CHAPTER ONE

CRIME SOMETIMES PAYS: but it has its casualties, too.

I was sitting behind a clear desk and smoking the last pipe of the day. Everything was tidy; my reports were in, and I was waiting only to give Dutt a lift to Tottenham. Since this was the new-New Scotland Yard I couldn't see the Thames from my window any more; but I could see, far away over the roofs, a row of tall, graceful steel storks, dipping and raising their intelligent beaks and performing slow ballet-movements among themselves: dock cranes. They assist my thinking when I'm engaged in a two-pipe problem. Because the street, on the other hand, fails to do this, I have had the bottom of the window masked with hard-board; and, still in pursuit of a climate for thought, have smuggled all my old furniture into this otherwise soulless cubicle. Fertile irregularity. Like the unofficial patina my pipe has begun to lay on the upper paintwork.

A moment of peace, with the blower resolutely silent: just the click of Dutt's typewriter from next door. But then a step in the passage and the door opening without a knock. Only one man does that: the Assistant Commissioner.

'Ah – Gently. Don't get up.'

I hadn't been going to. He whisked in.

'I've just come back from that Angry Brigade conference. Thought I had better look in if I was to catch you.'

He sat; he bowled me over with a smile.

'Are you feeling like a trip into the country?'

'It depends on the weather.'

'Capital. I have something here that will just suit you.'

When he beams like that, watch out. I moved my feet under the desk. Dutt's final barrage sounded off-stage, followed by the squeal of a sheet being whipped from a typewriter.

'Would that be Len?'

'I am waiting for him.'

'Call him in. He'll be going with you.'

I rose and obeyed. The A.C. exploited the interval by humming a snatch from *Pinafore*.

'Now look, you two. Frederick Albert Quarles. What do you know about that gentleman?'

Dutt looked at me for a lead.

'Isn't he the villain they call Flash Freddy?'

'The same.' The A.C. beamed at us. 'He's the boss of a snatch gang located in Hammersmith. The Met have been after him for four or five years. He has been one of their real headaches. Well, no longer. Freddy is dead. Apparently a confederate slipped a knife in him.'

'Have they got the man?'

'Yes. He is cooling his heels in a cell in Norchester.'

'Then where do we come in?'

'A simple double check. You are just to go over the locals' lines with them.'

Pause for gentle laughter.

I scratched a match for my pipe, which hardened the gleam in the A.C.'s eye. It is two years now since he gave up smoking, but the old Adam still twitches.

'Don't they have a case, then?'

'Of course they have a case. The fellow's name is Stanley Rampant. A local, he acted as a nose for Quarles. Freddy's gang had just done a job in Norchester. Rampant gave them the tip and Freddy set it up, but somebody put in a squeak to Met. The Met boys stopped the gang at a roadblock. They nicked four out of five of them, but missed the money.'

'How much?'

'Thirty-five thousand.'

I considered. 'Isn't Freddy a big operator?'

'One of the biggest. He may have slipped up this time. Perhaps Rampant's information wasn't reliable.'

'Then what happened?'

A comic shrug from the A.C. 'My guess is that Freddy wouldn't pay up. He gave Rampant a pourboire for expenses and told him he would have to try again. So buying it. They got on to Rampant through the car he had supplied for the getaway. It was clean, you see, it had to be legitimate. He gave a false name but the dealer knew him. When they nicked the mug he was still wearing the suit he had been wearing

3

when he killed Freddy. Blood-spots on the sleeve. He's a petty villain with minor form.'

'But he will have a story.'

'He says he got there second.'

'I can't see that inhibiting a jury.'

The A.C. made staccato popping sounds. 'Very well, then! Perhaps the case does have a few wrinkles. For one thing, somebody shopped the gang, and that somebody would scarcely have been Rampant. I.e. there was another villain around who wanted to put a spoke in Freddy's wheel. Then there are the injuries. He was badly cut up. There were thirteen stab-wounds in the back and neck. Any one of seven of them could have been fatal, and the rest weren't exactly acupunctures. How does that strike you?'

'Unprofessional.'

'A panicky amateur. Or else?'

'A hate killing.'

'Or else?'

'Cherchez la femme.'

'Aha.'

The A.C. had been selling it. And I'd bought it.

He pulled out some paper.

'Our dossier on Quarles. Freddy wasn't a common villain. Father a senior civil servant, deceased; a cousin in the Foreign Office, attached Washington. Prep school, Merchant Taylors', Magdalen, called to Bar '61, disbarred '64: interfered with witness in murder trial. Not convicted. No form. Associate of villains listed hereunder. Suspected complicity in fifty-six snatch jobs, proceeds totalling £2,357,025, in part

4

recovered. Alibi specialist. No person participating in robberies.'

I delivered a smoke-ring. 'A steady performer.'

'The Met boys won't shed any tears, sir,' Dutt said.

'Never mind that.' The A.C. waved at my smoke. 'Listen to what comes now. August '69 Quarles went to Paris. There was a snatch job done at the Renault works. No known complicity. What Quarles came back with was a Frenchwoman, Mimi Deslauriers. She has been living with him since then and she was staying with him in Norchester. Mimi Deslauriers, who was tried in Paris for the stabbing-to-death of her husband, Charles.' He rustled the paper. 'A nice coincidence?'

'I like the sound of Rampant better.'

'Neater, of course. It will please everyone. But meanwhile, Mimi has a lousy alibi.'

'Where were they staying?'

'At a place called the Barge-House. A riverside hotel outside Norchester.'

'Where was he killed?'

'He was killed in his car. It was parked on heath-land near the city.'

'What type of car?'

The A.C. gleamed again. 'Not your or my sort of car, Gently. He didn't get his sobriquet for nothing. The devil owned a Bugatti racer.'

'A which?'

'A Bugatti racer. One of those cars they sold to Maharajahs. A hundred and twenty in the shade. They were seeing off Bentleys when you were still at school.'

'It's an open two-seater?'

5

'Right. You must allow that Freddy had flair.'

'He would be wearing his shoulders handy for a knife.'

'Well, that sort of thing didn't happen to Louis Chiron.'

'Huh.' I stirred my feet. 'So Mimi is what's bothering them up there?'

'Principally Mimi. I hear she's flamboyant, is sort of giving the picture some colour. But don't overlook the other angle. Freddy must have made a lot of enemies. His just sitting back and using catspaws couldn't have made him terribly popular.'

'Who is handling the case?'

'Norchester and Mid-Northshire. But don't bother to phone them, I already have.' He dropped the paper on the desk. 'It's quite a simple case, really.'

'Oh quite,' I said. To the cranes.

He headed for his Bentley.

Dutt came round the desk and we skimmed through the bumf together.

'Len,' I said, leering at him. 'Len. Since when were you on first-name terms with His Nibs?'

Dutt coloured. 'He must have had my docs, sir.'

'And that means one of two things.'

'Well, I hope it's the right one, sir. With Terry going to Cambridge I could use the lolly.'

Six foot of cockney, that's Dutt. Born in Seven Sisters Road. Lifelong supporter of the Spurs, brown ale and small Fords. Not so much thick as slow: he's got a brain that won't be hurried. Hence missing preferment's eye. Preferment being the loser.

'Then we had better make a good impression with this one. I can get you a mug-shot in the local press.'

'Don't suppose His Nibs will see it.'

'You are underestimating His Nibs.'

As I chanced to know, one of His Nibs' disbursements went to a cuttings agency in Chancery Lane. No press acquired by a Central Office lackey escaped the eye of Big Brother.

Along with the CR mish were copies of photographs of Quarles (all highly confidential, of course, since Quarles had never been convicted). A handsome, long-featured man with a romantic black mane, smiling dark eyes, set close, and thin lips parted over ferret's teeth. Forty-five. Slim, tallish. Spoke with a public school accent. Charm that triggered-off women. A numbered bank-account; a Bugatti.

'Would you buy a used car from him?'

Dutt sniggered. 'He wouldn't be selling my kind of car.'

'I'm keen to see his choice in women.'

'Bet you she looks like Ursula Andress.'

The address given was a flat in Upper Cheyne Row ('Where they half-inched the posh paving-stones': Dutt), and alongside the Bugatti he had run a Citroën Pallas: for when it rained, no doubt.

Attached to the rest, a résumé of the snatch job and the Met C.I.D.'s commendable action. The villains involved were named Norton, Elsing, Wicken, Lound and Fring. A specialist mob. They all had form; three had done time for GBH. Fring was the one who had got away, taking with him the loot in a black suitcase.

Named i/c case, Chief Inspector Dainty. The switch-board got him at the third attempt.

Burning question: 'Who gave you the tip-off?'

Dainty's answers were evasive.

'A regular?'

'Not as far as we know.'

'Man or woman?'

'We think it was a man.'

'You are not sure?'

'Pretty certain. But he was talking through his scarf.'

'When did it come through?'

'At fifteen-five. We only just had time to set up the block.'

'How did you come to lose Fring?'

'They pulled up short of us. Fring was out of the car like a rabbit. He hooked on to a bus turning out of a junction. By the time we stopped it he had vanished.'

They had had a dust-up with the other four, no doubt laid on to give Fring his start. Fring, of course, was removing the evidence. It was tucked away in the black suitcase.

'What are you holding them on?'

'An offensive weapon charge. But that will change when we catch Fring. We have a stake-out at his house in Battersea and a watch on all his known haunts.'

'Well, he won't be strapped for a night's lodging.'

Dainty's laugh sounded sour. 'We have had information coming in. I don't think you need worry about Fring.'

I nagged him again about the tip-off, which had

come from a call-box. The informant had named two of the men, Lound and Fring, and had referred to the gang as 'Flash Freddy's mob'. He had also described the car accurately, except for transposing numerals in the registration.

'A local call?'

'No way of telling.'

'Who would have it in for Flash Freddy?'

'That's what the snouts aren't telling us. When they do, you will be informed.'

I hung up and exchanged looks with Dutt, who had been listening on the extension.

'So. What do we make of that?'

He rumpled his face. 'It beats me, sir. It can't have been Rampant who put the squeak in. He'd be cutting his own throat.'

'Suppose he had reasons.'

'Like what, sir?'

'Like trying to put the squeeze on Freddy.'

Dutt shook his homely bonce. 'Wouldn't be a sensible thing to do, sir.'

No, it wouldn't. But villains are stupid, especially little-leaguers like Rampant. And if it wasn't Rampant who put in the squeak, then we were groping around already.

Ah, well. Blessings on snouts.

'First thing in the morning then, Dutt.'

'Perhaps we'll have had a tinkle by then, sir.'

I'm not an optimist, but I like them round me.

Living my life, and not theirs, I spent the evening with Brenda Merryn. Why aren't we married? We prefer it that way, and Brenda would make a wretched housewife. It was May and sweet weather so we took a stroll along the Embankment, had a couple of drinks at her favourite pub, then returned to her flat to grill two steaks.

With Brenda, I am indiscreet (she first came my way as a murder suspect). I mentioned Flash Freddy's sad end, introducing the Bugatti and Mimi Deslauriers.

'She's a raving blonde,' Brenda said promptly.

'Is this psychic vision or have you seen her?'

'Seen her, met her, watched her operate. I've always moved in exalted circles.'

Which didn't altogether surprise me. Brenda works in Chelsea and has friends and a relative there.

'Where did you meet her?'

'At one of Siggy's parties. He never did sail round the world, you know. She's a busty bitch with a snub nose and dimples. If you disappear I shall know what has happened.'

'She was accused of stabbing her first husband.'

'Ha,' Brenda said. 'Then watch your back. I was going round telling myself all evening that Mimi Deslauriers had probably stabbed her first husband.'

'Was Quarles with her?'

'Tall, dark and sneaky?'

'That's the man.'

'He was there. He made a teeny-weeny little pass at me, and then keeled over when she looked at him.'

'She was jealous.'

'Possessive.'

'What about him?'

'I don't think he had much say in the matter. Mimi

was lining them up in a queue, but that was her prerogative. Not Sneaky's.'

'Interesting.'

Brenda went out and returned wearing something more comfortable. I got back to Elphinstone Road at about ohone-hundred hours: not the best of preparations for a trip to the country.

CHAPTER TWO

N O TINKLE IN the morning. Just an electricity bill and a letter in pencil, signed Justice: a threat to bomb the Bank of England unless we released a felon called Dakin. Worth a try, I suppose. I made arrangements to have it collected. Outside, a brilliant day, with a scent of lime-flowers coming from the Gardens.

Dutt arrived in time to drink coffee. We fetched my Lotus from the garage and locked up his Escort. Dutt had been brooding over the tip-off mystery and had reached the conclusion that, after all, the squeaker must have been Rampant.

'It's the timing, sir. It had to come from someone who knew the job had been pulled. Then there's the car, he knew all about that. Even got the number nearly right.'

'Rampant bought the car. Wouldn't he have got it quite right?'

'It couldn't have been long in his possession, sir. And me, I always have to think twice when I'm asked for my number.'

Well. But if Rampant had planned a tip-off, he would surely have made a note of the number. Also, he would probably have named all the gang. The message to Met had been less than explicit.

'It might have been a snap decision by Rampant, but more likely it was a grass from some other ill-wisher.'

'But how did they know about the car, sir?'

'Simple. They saw it. Crooks can put on a tail as well as we can.'

'You mean someone was out there keeping tabs on Freddy?'

'Right. And with luck he'll have left a trail.'

'So like that it could have a connection with the killing?'

I grinned. 'Get in the car. We'll go and find out.'

Driving fast.

We picked up the A1 and switched to the A505 at Baldock. The Lotus's virtues are wasted on dual carriageways and their semi-legal eighty. Jigging by puffing transporters, swooping round coveys of hard-driving reps. Slinking through bends with a steady clock. Here and there brushing the ton. The Lotus is a naughty car which has always a train to catch somewhere. Dutt, the perfect passenger, loves it: sits loose and dreamy, watching the road perpetually opening for us.

'Wonder what that Bugatti's like to drive, sir.'

I nod. 'It's been crossing my mind, too.'

Dutt gives me a glance. 'Perhaps we'll get a whirl in it.'

'Perhaps,' I say, savouring my hypocrisy.

We slotted in at Norchester police H.Q., which is a wing of the big, pinkish City Hall. The press were waiting outside and I introduced Dutt to them as our leading expert on knife-killings. They took appropriate photographs. Then we were ushered in to the office of C.I.D. Chief Inspector Hanson. This was my fourth time with Hanson, who is not an unmixed admirer of mine. But today he was affable enough; I believe he thought he had the case licked.

'Rampant's going to crack.'

'That will be nice.'

Hanson flicked his grey eyes at me. Hack-faced Hanson. He's not so tough really; there's a soft centre under the chromium plate.

'He's admitted he was after his cut. Quarles brushed him off with two hundred nicker. Quarles would never have seen him again unless Rampant was threatening him. Chummie's got no answer to that one.'

'Where is Rampant now?'

'I've got him downstairs.' Hanson hesitated. 'Do you want to have a go at him?'

'First, you'd better put me in the picture.'

'Yeah, well. It makes quite a story.'

We seated ourselves. Also in the office was Hanson's lieutenant, Sergeant Opie, a short, solid, dark-haired man with an empty face but alert eyes.

'Let's start at the beginning. Whose money was it?'

Hanson gave a little snatch with his head. 'Bryanston Shoes. Big footwear people. They have a factory on the outskirts.'

14

'Wages?'

'Yep. They draw them on Thursdays to give the clerks time to make them up. Collect them at Lloyd's branch on The Walk. The car, driver, and one guard.'

'Just one guard?'

'One guard. And don't think we haven't talked to them about security. But this is Norchester, not London. Here they don't believe it till it happens.'

'What about their route?'

'They use two, through the centre and by Unwin Road. The trouble is they just alternate them, one this week, the other the next. So they were sitters for a villain like Quarles. He set it up at the quiet end of Unwin Road.'

'How long had Quarles been in the district?'

'He was out at the Barge-House all week. It's on the river, you know, a holiday spot. Quarles just acted as though he were on holiday.'

'Where was he when the job was pulled?'

'In a launch on the river, along with his woman and two others they'd invited. When we heard from Met we went out and questioned him, but he just laughed in our bloody faces. Then the next evening, he was dead.'

'Tell me about that.'

Hanson heaved rough breath. He pulled open a drawer, took out a folder and slid it to me across the desk. The photographs. Not very pretty, but I've spent much of my lifetime studying such things. They showed Flash Freddy with a faceful of steering-wheel and a ventilated back and a bloody neck. Also the car, the lovely car. It was standing on a rough track, surrounded by trees. Just where it was parked was a large, jungly hawthorn with bracken growing round its skirts.

'Where was this?'

'Part of Mussel Heath. It flanks the city to the north.'

'It looks more like a wood.'

'There's plenty of cover there. No doubt why chummie picked it for a meeting.'

'Give me the timetable.'

'Quarles left the hotel around twenty hundred hours Friday evening. It's a seven-mile drive. E.T.D. between twenty hundred hours and midnight. Reported oh-eight-twenty-five Saturday by Samuel Trivett, labourer. Trivett lives in a road adjacent to the heath, was taking his dog for a stroll.'

'Wasn't Quarles reported missing by Madame Deslauriers?'

'Nope.'

'Did you ask her why?'

'You bet I asked her. She said that Quarles had gone out on business, and when that happened she expected him when she saw him.'

I hesitated. 'Did she know what business?'

'If she did, she's not admitting it.'

'Where was she during the rest of that evening?'

'In her room is what she says.'

'But no proof?'

Hanson swept his bony hand. 'All right, I thought about that! But I couldn't believe it. Not with the lab report coming in about Rampant's jacket, and him with a motive as big as a house. Believe me, I know that bastard – he could do it and not lose any sleep.'

16

Perhaps, perhaps. I pointed to the photographs. 'Nobody's mentioned the weapon yet.'

Hanson got red. 'Because we haven't found it. I'd say chummie took it with him and threw it in the river.'

'Do we know what it was like?'

'Yes, a short-bladed knife, blade not longer than four inches. A straight back with a curved edge. Could be a small kitchen knife.'

'Commonly of French manufacture.'

'Yeah, well! That's a point. But you can buy them here in town, so I don't see where that gets us.'

I hunched. 'Had the body been frisked?'

'If it had, the chummie missed five hundred nicker.'

Hanson lifted a plastic bag from his drawer and decanted its contents on the desk. Out came a fat wallet, keys, change, pens, a platinum cigarette-case, matching lighter, pen-knife, nail-file, comb and a rabbit's foot. I chivvied them around. The cigarette-case and lighter may have been worth another five hundred. In the wallet, mostly twenty-pound notes, bank-fresh, very handsome. Driving-licence, virgin. Insurance and M.O.T. certificates for 3.3 litre Bugatti (1932). Membership card the Dolly Club, Chelsea, receipt for jacket (£132.13), stamps, three credit cards, two theatre-ticket stubs, two gilt-edged visiting cards.

'Personal jewellery?'

Hanson opened an initialled envelope. 'These came back from the mortuary.'

He shook out a Longines watch with a platinum case and expanding band and a solitaire diamond ring in the same metal.

'Clothes?'

Hanson signalled to Opie, who fetched another bag, from a metal cabinet. He spread out a grey light-weight suit, silk shirt, socks and underwear and a pair of handmade shoes in natural camel-skin. The shirt and jacket were ripped and stained: very butcher-like exhibits.

'A well-turned-out corpse.'

'Yeah,' Hanson said. 'You'd have thought he was worth taking away.'

'Somebody just wanted him dead.'

'Somebody like Rampant.'

'But wasn't Rampant's quarrel with him about cash?'

Hanson made noises. 'So the chummie panicked. Hell, he wasn't so relaxed when he spoiled that shirt. Perhaps something disturbed him, like a car passing close. There's a lot of necking goes on out there.'

I grunted. 'It'll keep till I've viewed the scene. Now tell me something about Mimi Deslauriers.'

Hanson rolled his eyes. 'It'll be a pleasure. But if you think she's chummie, you must be slipping.'

He lit one of his cheroots, long, black, and puffed coarse smoke over my head.

'Around thirty,' he said. 'Blonde. Green eyes. Say thirty-six, twenty-four, thirty-six. Tallish. Moves like a cat. Husky voice with an accent. Nearly knocks you down when she looks at you. Fancy dresser. Smells like honey.'

'I'll recognize her,' I said. 'Where was she on Friday evening?'

He leached smoke. 'In her room. She went up after dinner, after Quarles left.'

'And stayed there?'

'That's what she says. Had a bath and went to bed.' Hanson's eyes were dreamy. 'It's a hell of a world,' he said.

'Any corroboration?'

'None.'

'Does the room have a phone?'

'Not an outside line.'

'Could she have left unnoticed?'

'With a lot of luck. You can get down backstairs to the kitchen end.'

'Does she have alternative transport?'

'Nothing we know about. But there'd be a rush if she wanted to borrow some. Only it's crazy, quite crazy. That doll wouldn't have to murder anyone.'

I threw him an empty look. 'They did tell you her form?'

He pulled in a contemptuous lungful. 'Sure, sure. But she got off, didn't she? That was just her bit of hard luck.'

'And this would be another bit?'

'Why not? She's the sort of dame things happen around. But if she sneaked out and filled-in Quarles, I'll eat a year's supply of these things.'

Well . . . he'd met her, and I hadn't. 'What was her reaction to the killing?'

'She was concerned, you could say that. But she wasn't washing out her hankie.'

'Scared?'

'Could have been scared. She was all round me with a lot of questions.'

'About what you were thinking?'

'That sort of thing. I didn't get the impression it was the end of her world.'

'So Quarles was just another mug.'

Hanson scowled through his smoke. 'Why should she break her heart over a jerk like that?'

We drank coffee, the canteen kind, then drove out to Mussel Heath. I had seen it before, on a previous case, but just to admire it in passing. The city fingers its suburbs into the edge of the heath, which rises above it in broken lines; from up there the city is mapped below you with its landmarks of churches, tower-blocks, the castle and the cathedral. The heath is a hilly and holey place where you could lose an armoured division. Parts are open, parts scrubby and wooded, with precipitous dells and overgrown hollows. It is criss-crossed by stony tracks, going nowhere in particular, and divided by a road that snakes up to join a ring-road.

We arrived by the dividing road. It rose beside a bare hill-slope, topped by an empty Victorian barracks; passed some pre-war council estates, then wound its way fenceless into high, woody heath. Hanson pulled into an official parking-place; from the far side a track dipped sharply; we bumbled down it, brushing bracken and birch-twigs, and levelled off in one of the dells. Another hundred yards brought us to the hawthorn which I had noticed in the photographs. We climbed out. Hanson pointed to four pegs hammered firmly into the ground.

'That's where Quarles parked his heap. A nice, quiet spot for a villains' conference.'

'But how would Quarles know about it?'

'Rampant showed it to him. This is where he gave Freddy the dope. Freddy wasn't keen on being seen with Rampant, so he picked him up at the parking-place and drove down here.'

'Does Rampant admit that?'

'Sure. He's given us the whole tale as far as the hold-up. Then we know that Rampant called Freddy here for a second meeting. It's after that when the edges get blurred.'

I poked around. The sides of the dell were fledged with tall-growing birches and sycamores. Where we'd come down was hidden by a turn and the dell came to an end just past the hawthorn. The ground was stony and didn't take tracks. There were a couple of footpaths leading off. One climbed out at the end of the dell, the other at the side, starting by the hawthorn. I scrambled up the latter. It took me nowhere, just through the trees into open heath. I came down again; and paused for some moments beside the hawthorn, which was in flower.

'Give me your version of what happened.'

'Huh?' Hanson stared scowlingly. 'There's only one version I know about. Rampant got Quarles to meet him here, didn't he?'

'But then?'

'Then he'd get in the jalopy beside him, start trying to pressure him to cough up.'

'Go on.'

'So Quarles wouldn't play, so there was a barney and Rampant pulled a knife. If he was planning to put the black on Quarles, he'd have been a mug to come bare-handed.'

'And all this took place in the cockpit of a Bugatti?'

Hanson held back, glowering. 'You reckon it couldn't have?'

'I reckon there wasn't much room to draw a knife, and none to use it in the way it was used. Is Rampant some sort of Samson?'

'Not so as you'd notice.'

'Then he wasn't in the car when he stabbed Quarles. He couldn't have put the knife in once, not reaching round Quarles while sitting beside him.'

Hanson looked savage. 'So how did he do it?'

'I think Quarles' attacker came round this bush. He jammed Quarles' face into the wheel with one hand while he stabbed his back with the other.'

'Oh fine,' Hanson said. 'Very clever.'

'Which suggests something vital about the attacker. He is probably left-handed. Is Rampant left-handed?'

Hanson glared awhile. Then he got in the car.

CHAPTER THREE

S O FAR SO good: I felt now I had earned a look at the
Bugatti. We drove back to H.Q. in silence, then I
put my request to Hanson.

We found the Bugatti sitting in a corner of the
H.Q. garage, reverentially draped in a plastic dust-
sheet. Lab had finished with it. Most of Quarles'
bleeding had been soaked up by his clothing. A few
smears on the wheel and the white leather bucket-
seat had been photographed then cleaned off, while the
recognizable latents were either Quarles' or off-record,
probably innocent.

Hanson called over a mech. The mech started it
for us and drove it out into the yard. It stood there
growling in a chesty way, like a leopard meditating
its spring. A marvellous blue shape. Beginning at the
rad, an ellipse perhaps borrowed from Leonardo da
Vinci; carried on through the delicate humping of the
louvred bonnet, completed in the powerful signature
of the fish-tail. Ettore had reached for one of Plato's
patterns, and it had come to his hand like a pint pot.

'What's the price of a heap like this?' Hanson asked.

I didn't hear him; I was walking round it. Whatever Flash Freddy's sins had been, I felt I owed him gratitude for the Bugatti. The French racing-blue enamel was stove-hard everywhere, no hint of rust or tarnish. The cockpit appointments were immaculately original, so too were the strap-spoked aluminium wheels. The seats were new, but gave immediate conviction that they had been scrupulously copied from the originals. And the note of the engine, a precise, clear grumble, needed no connoisseur to confirm its tune.

The mech gently revved it, bringing in the supercharger. Faces appeared at a few nearby windows. Other mechs, who had been working in the garage, came out to stare at Ettore's car.

Rampant wasn't left-handed.

I had ordered coffee before they fetched him to the office. When I offered him a cup, he shifted it to his left hand and then stirred it with his right.

A frightened little villain. Aged about thirty, five-foot-seven, slim build; a blotchy ferret-face, long, lank fair hair and a soupy, unwashed appearance. Dress, a scruffy sweater, poncy jacket, dirty jeans and cheap suede sneakers.

A petty villain; mostly a nuisance; sometimes useful to the villainocracy.

'You knew Frederick Quarles, Rampant?'

'Well yes, I had to, didn't I?'

'Where did you meet him?'

'Well, I didn't sort of know him, just met a bloke who was working for him.'

'Where?'

'Well, in the nick, wasn't it?'

'I'm asking you.'

'Yeah, in the nick.'

'What was his name?'

'It was Wickey, wasn't it? Him what was in there for knocking-off cars.'

'Are you referring to Alfred Wicken?'

'Bleeding Wickey is all I know. Wish I'd never listened to the frigger. Wouldn't've been here now, would I?'

He lapped up coffee, hands a-tremble. Very scared was Stanley Rampant.

'What did he want?'

Rampant clattered the cup and saucer. 'Said I could be a nose for a big boy, didn't he? Wasn't no risk, it was money for jam. Just give him a tinkle when I was on to something.'

'And you tipped him off about the Bryanston wages collection.'

'Well yes, I did, didn't I?'

'Then you actually met Quarles.'

'Yeah, all right, I met him. I ain't trying to hide nothing, I'm being straight.'

Straight as a meat-hook.

'What happened at that meeting?'

Rampant clutched cup and saucer together. 'Bleeding business, that's what it was. You can't make nothing else of it.'

'Quarles gave you money?'

'Yeah, for the car—'

'Just for the car?'

25

'Ain't I bleeding telling you! He gave me the price of a '65 Jag and a bundle for me, isn't that right?'

'How much for you?'

'He give me a bundle.'

'How much?'

'Two hundred nicker!'

I clicked my tongue. 'That wasn't much, Stanley. I would have reckoned your cut at about fifteen hundred.'

'Yeah, but that was on account—!'

'On account of what?'

Rampant juggled with the cup, got coffee on his jeans.

'It was on account of what you'd get from the share-out,' I said. 'Only there wasn't any share-out. The two hundred was all.'

Dutt divested him of the cup and saucer. Rampant's blotches were mottling unhealthily. Too many belly-fuls of crisps and beer and morning lie-ins with the tarts. I let him sweat while I skimmed through his statement, a tiresome document in policese. Then I lit my pipe. He was watching me hungrily; there were yellow stains on his shaking fingers.

'Want a fag, Rampant?'

'Yeah. Yeah, I want one.'

I nodded. 'Tell me what happened Friday evening.'

His eyes glazed. 'You got it down there.'

'Not what I want to hear from you, Rampant.'

'It's the truth, isn't it?'

'Not all the truth. Quarles didn't just meet you for a social chat. I want to know what it was that fetched him there. What you had to say to each other.'

'But we didn't say nothing—!'

'What fetched him there?'

'I don't bleeding know! He was dead, wasn't he?'

'Then why did you want to meet him?'

'I frigging didn't. It was his idea.'

'He rang you to arrange it?'

'That's right!'

Hanson said: 'You're not on the phone, you stupid bastard.'

'So like it was a message, then – yeah, a note—'

'And you're a pig's arse,' Hanson said.

Rampant breathed fast. I mouthed a smoke-ring.

'Listen,' I said. 'You're in a hole, Rampant. Your part in the wage-snatch was worth a twicer. But unless you help us to come up with a better answer, that blood on your sleeve could make it life. Is that what you want?'

'I never killed Freddy.'

'There's nobody else under suspicion.'

'But I frigging didn't!'

'Who's going to believe you?'

'They got to believe me!'

'Shit,' Hanson said.

Rampant whimpered, screwing himself away from us. Suddenly he looked about fifteen. He'd got thick, ugly hands and bony wrists. Just a nasty little kid with a too-old face.

He moaned. 'I wanted my pay-off.'

'Now he tells us,' Hanson sneered.

'He was dead. He was frigging dead. It's true. He was all over blood when I got there.'

'Just you and him.'

'I wanted my cut. It wasn't my fault the job went wrong.'

'So you put the black on him.'

'It was what he owed me.'

'Oh Christ,' Hanson said. 'They come thicker and thicker.'

I signalled to Dutt; he gave Rampant a fag. Rampant's mouth quivered as he dragged on it. Hanson stuffed a cheroot into his own mouth and sat gazing hood-eyed at Rampant.

So now Rampant was giving.

I took him through his statement detail by detail, trying to squeeze out some small fact that would give us a hint, a direction. But Rampant didn't know much. His contact with the gang had stopped short at Wicken and Quarles; the Bryanston job was his first tip-off: he had stepped up a league to come an immediate cropper. Still, I kept leaning on him. We worked through the wage-snatch and came to his phone-call to Quarles on the Friday. Rampant was sweating. This was the part he'd got to get us to believe somehow.

'What happened on Friday?'

'Well, on Friday I saw the papers, didn't I?'

'You saw the papers and phoned Quarles.'

'Yeah, I wanted to know what was going on.'

'And Quarles was happy about you phoning him?'

'No, he bleeding wasn't! He chewed me up, told me I'd got to forget I'd ever heard of him.'

'Then you threatened to grass.'

'Well, he asked for it, didn't he? It wasn't like he

hadn't got the loot. One of his blokes dodged off with it. I'd read all that in the papers.'

'Who suggested the meeting?'

'Like I did.'

'And Quarles agreed?'

'Bleeding had to, hadn't he? I'd got my monkey up. All he wanted was to get me off the frigging phone.'

'He didn't shout back at you?'

'No, he never. He was talking like he'd got a cop at his elbow.'

'There was someone with him?'

'Well, talking like that. But bleeding nasty, all the same.'

Point to check at the Barge-House.

'What time was this?'

'Oh Christ knows. Maybe half-past ten, eleven.'

'Where were you phoning from?'

'The box near my flat.'

'Just you on your tod?'

'Yeah, I'm telling you.'

The meeting had been timed for eight-thirty p.m. He had spent the rest of the day in agitation. Successive editions of the evening papers made no mention of Fring's having been arrested. At opening-time he'd gulped down two pints at his local, but swore he hadn't mentioned the meeting to anyone. From seven-thirty to eight-fifteen he'd been alone in his flat. Then he'd got in his car and driven to the heath.

'Nobody tailed you?'

'I wouldn't know, would I? I had to go all through the city.'

'What about where you go up by the barracks?'

'Wasn't nobody behind me there.'

So he'd arrived at the parking-place and parked there. Several other cars were present, but not the Bugatti. Rampant had waited a few minutes in case Quarles was late, then he'd set off to the rendezvous on foot.

'Can you remember those other cars?'

Rampant dusted sweat. 'I see a couple smooching in a red A40. Then there was a Cort parked next to me. And a clapped-out Consul, all over stickers.'

'Did you notice anyone sitting in them, apart from the couple?'

Rampant shook his head reluctantly.

'What colour was the Consul?'

'Black, I reckon.'

'And the Cortina?'

'Green. A Mark 2.'

And there had been six or seven cars more, of which he remembered not a single feature.

'Let's take it slowly, now. You went down that track, from which there's a good view round about. What did you see?'

'Well nothing, did I? It's just a lot of trees and sort of ferns.'

'Think carefully. Did you hear anything?'

'There were cars going along the road.'

'No sounds from below?'

His ferret eyes were helpless. 'Honest. I never heard a thing.'

'All right. Keep going.'

His mouth quavered. 'So I come round the corner and see the car. At first I think the bleeder's dozed off, that's how it looks, him hung over the wheel. Then I come up. His frigging arm is dangling and there's blood all over his back. So I gets hold of the bastard and tries to pull him up. Then I can see he's bloody deado.'

'Did you see a knife?'

'There wasn't no knife.'

'Sure?'

'Of course I bleeding am! If there was a knife it wasn't stuck in him. I ain't saying it wasn't around.'

'Did you touch or move anything?'

'No I never. I just got out of there sharp.'

'You heard, saw, nobody?'

'I keep telling you, don't I? I never see nobody at all.'

I fed him another fag, then we went through it once again. Nothing fresh, except now he remembered two more of the cars, a Minx and a Herald. By this time Rampant was drying-up, so I let them march him back to the cells. His information had been mostly negative: but that can be important, too.

Five minutes' thought, while Hanson fumigated his office with a fresh cheroot. He had been quiet during the later stages of my examination of Rampant. Now he hosed smoke at me.

'So what's the verdict from the big man?'

I slid him a grin. 'Better tell me yours. You've been longer on the case.'

'I've seen more of Rampant.'

'Granted.'

'That bastard's been in my hair a long time. He's

31

owing for six or seven jobs that I know about but can't pin on him.'

'One of the facts of life.'

'Yeah. And now I've got the sod dangling. You could do me an Old Pals' Act and he would be out of my hair for good.'

'Is that what you're suggesting?'

'I'm bloody tempted. Except I know you won't play. And except I've been listening to you turning him over, and I'm not so sure about him any more.'

'He's still the lad with the blood on his sleeve.'

'Yeah, but he was telling his story better. At times I was almost just going to believe him, had to keep reminding myself he was Rampant.'

I got up. 'Too soon,' I said. 'We may circle round and come back to Rampant. It could be that he saw that job done, even though he didn't use the knife himself.'

Hanson huffed smoke. 'Is that your verdict?'

I hunched a shoulder. 'Rampant will keep. Meanwhile I have another appointment.'

Hanson nodded slowly. 'And she smells sweeter.'

CHAPTER FOUR

R AMPANT WASN'T LEFT-HANDED: which helped his case, though it didn't exonerate him. On the other hand, I knew he wasn't Dainty's squeaker the first time he opened his mouth. He spoke with a Norchester street-accent, a debased form of the more vigorous Northshire; no Met officer would have missed it, though Rampant had talked through a dozen scarves.

In fact, Dainty had made no mention of accent: a negative point that was slightly suggestive. What accent, or nuance, wouldn't register with a Met man? Quick answer: his own. Thus the squeaker most likely was a Londoner, though not one with a coarsely cockney accent. A man indifferently educated, perhaps a rival gang-leader – in which case the snouts should be able to finger him.

Though they hadn't, yet. My next move was to ring Dainty, who had no news: he sounded uffish.

Lunch. I invited Hanson, but he had got hung up with some petty villainery – two chummies who were impersonating council rent-collectors, and making a good thing of it. I took Dutt to The Princess, a cellar-like establishment in the neighbourhood of the provision market, known to me from that early case involving a Dutch timber-importer and his ingenious manager. The Princess had changed little that I could see. The same dimly-lit cosiness and competent waitresses. We had their mixed grill followed by gateau, and the years had altered the quality of neither.

'Done any thinking?' I asked Dutt.

'No sir. Excepting I don't like Rampant.'

'You don't think he came clean?'

'That's the trouble, sir. I've a nasty feeling that he did.'

'So leaving the field open.'

Dutt chewed and nodded. 'I reckon it's a queer old job altogether. I can see another villain putting a squeak in, but knocking off Freddy would be just stupid.'

'Especially the way it was done.'

'Exactly, sir. It isn't the style of our villains. They'd have picked up Freddy coming out of a pub, not tailed him out to no heath.'

'Somebody with more than a professional motive.'

'Yes, but the snouts would know about that, sir. And we don't hear nothing. I'm getting the notion the bloke we're looking for is a strict amateur.'

I gnawed some liver. 'Yet there was a squeak. The professionals come into the act somewhere.'

We ate up and paid. Our waitress was elderly, and my vanity hoped that she might remember me. She didn't, of course. I was just a stranger, betrayed by the unwonted size of my tip.

I collected the Lotus and we drove out of Norchester by a route made unfamiliar by one-way systems. The Barge-House was at Haughton St John (pronounced Hoffen-John by Hanson), a riverside village eight miles distant. This too I had known in past times; it is a sort of hire-boat metropolis. But in autumn, when the motor-cruisers have stopped knocking value off each other, it is also a station for pike and bream.

The road led through a gentle, paintable country of suave undulations and psychic trees, with once a glimpse of a square flint tower to give a fix in centuries. Followed the ribbon-development of half-comely Wrackstead, which lives across the river from Haughton; and finally the vandalized humpback bridge, a victim of traffic and official callousness.

A few years ago you could have parked by the bridge while you strolled back to admire the boating scene. Now you crawled over a bumping Bailey structure to be marshalled through yellow lines to a suicidal crossways. One of the roads I remembered had vanished, its place taken by a sprawling Superstore. Another had been widened in an unlovely way, hastening more traffic to the inevitable jam. No logic, no way out, except possibly a surgical use of the bomb. Many years behind need the local authorities would doubtless concede a new river-crossing.

We negotiated the jam, then turned left into a road that paralleled the river. The Barge-House, an Edwardian pub enlarged into a hotel, occupied a site opposite to a bank. It was a heavy, redbrick building, set flush to the pavement, with a small forecourt intended for horse-gigs; also a yard to one side, which was presently resembling a car-dealer's lot. Not a lovesome place; but what you didn't see was that it had lawns running through to the river. A sign-board, not yet modernized, offered launches, skiffs and rowboats for hire.

I parked and sat appraising the scene. The road was called Bylore Road. Traffic was queued all along it, waiting to break into the chaos at the crossroads. Adjacent to the Barge-House were three sad terrace cottages, apparently built with bricks left over; then a slightly more engaging, white-plastered building, exhibiting the sign of Three Tuns. I nudged Dutt.

'Think like a villain who wants to keep an eye on Flash Freddy.'

Dutt grinned. 'He couldn't have hired the bank, sir.'

'So go buy yourself a pint before the bar closes.'

Dutt went. I parked the Lotus in the forecourt, where there was space beside a badge-heavy Alfa. Two good-looking cars: though one had stood there lately which – for looks – would have smeared either into the woodwork.

The exterior of the Barge-House did it an injustice; once through the swing-doors things became plusher. You stepped into a long hall with concealed wall-lighting, a spongy carpet and a smell of old brandy. Left was the reception office: empty. I pressed the bell-push and waited. Across the end of the hall passed deft young waiters, presumably en route between kitchen and dining-room. A door to the bar was opposite the office and from that way came conversation, clinking and laughter. Finally, from kitchenwards, hurried a man in a lounge-suit. He glided up to me, smiling apologetically.

'So sorry to keep you. We've been busy.'

'Mr Frayling?'

'What can I do for you?'

'Shall we go in the office?'

His smile slipped a notch; but only for a moment. We went into the office.

Frayling was the manager. He had guessed who I was, but I told him all the same. He was a slim, willowy type, mid-forties, a lined face and conciliatory eyes. Somehow he suggested to me a busted schoolmaster, but I didn't go into his record. He flicked the glass shutter across the reception window and we sat down on two well-padded chairs.

'I'm here about the killing, not the robbery, though there's a probable connection. I intend to make the hotel my base. I'll need rooms for myself and my Inspector.'

'Of course, I'd like to help you, but—'

'Good. You can begin by booking us in.'

He shrugged but pulled over the register. A couple of the existing guests got shunted.

'Now tell me about Quarles.'

Frayling's eyes jumped. 'I – I made a full statement to Inspector Hanson.'

'I know.' I patted the brief-case I had with me. 'And now I want to hear it at first-hand. Have you any objection?'

'No, of course not!'

'You had no connection with Quarles, for instance?'

'Good lord, no!'

'Then give me a quick run through. I'd like to know why he chose the Barge-House.'

Frayling couldn't tell me that, and the point was probably of no importance. But it got Frayling going on the wrong foot, which is the first move in interrogation. Quarles had booked by phone a fortnight ahead, no doubt when he'd received the tip from Rampant. He had booked for a week, from Saturday to Saturday, just like any other vacationist. He had arrived at mid-day, making some stir with his car and his companion. Frayling had given them his best room, overlooking the river. Quarles had registered Mimi as his wife.

'Were you happy about that?'

Frayling's smirk was edgy. 'I can't ask too many questions, can I? Most of our guests are married couples. You take them on trust if it isn't too obvious.'

'Wasn't this obvious?'

'No, I wouldn't have said so. Even ladies like this one can get married. And they were matter-of-fact enough with each other, they'd obviously been together for a while.'

'Matter-of-fact?'

'I think that describes it. They weren't rushing to jump into bed. Actually, I was wondering if they'd had a tiff. But they were just the same later on.'

Interesting.

'Did they have any quarrels?'

'No. Not to my knowledge.'

'Displays of jealousy?'

'She could be catty, but there wasn't any real venom behind it.'

'What about Quarles?'

Frayling fidgeted. 'I have to admit that I rather liked him. He was a well-educated man, you know, very polite, a lot of charm. But subdued, that's how he struck me. As though he might have some sadness in his background. I was never more taken aback in my life than when I learned he was a crook.'

'Did *he* show any jealousy?'

'He wasn't easy to read. He had that sort of public-school veneer. But it didn't seem to bother him what the lady got up to. I suppose he must have been used to her winsome ways.'

I stared. 'Tell me about them.'

Frayling hefted his neat shoulders. 'Don't forget she is still a guest here.'

'And don't you forget we're talking about murder.'

He sulked a bit; flipped the leaves of the register. 'All right. But don't let on that I told you. Anything in trousers was getting an eye from her. Some of the wives here weren't so tranquil.'

'How far did it go?'

'I don't think it went anywhere. The lady is just fond of exciting attention.'

'Was she needling Quarles?'

Frayling hesitated. 'I don't think I'm qualified to pronounce on that.'

'So he just took it in good part.'

'Yes, as far as I could see. But like I said, he wasn't easy to read. A quiet sort of character. He would sit chatting racing while the lady was preening herself with the men.'

'Quiet.'

'Yes.'

Well, he'd have things on his mind; which weren't necessarily connected with Mimi Deslauriers.

I fetched up my brief-case.

'Then from what you're saying, neither Quarles nor Deslauriers were particularly stand-offish.'

Frayling nodded. 'They were both good mixers. Quarles arranged several picnics to go on the river.'

'Any special friends?'

'None I noticed. I can give you some names of the people they invited.'

'Did you notice if there was anyone they specially avoided?'

He shook his head. 'I don't think so.'

'Did they have any visitors?'

'Not to my knowledge. But of course, strangers use the public rooms. The saloon and bar are packed every night. It goes on like that till late September.'

'People off the boats?'

'Mostly from the boats. Some of them drive out here from town. Then you get day-trippers in from the coast. We have a big turnover of casuals.'

'Anyone like this?'

I took out a mug-shot of Rampant, part of the bumf I'd collected from Hanson. Frayling stared at it curiously, but apparently it didn't ring a bell.

'You'd better show that to the bar-tenders. I'm not often in the bar. Who is he?'

'It doesn't matter.' I returned the photograph to the brief-case. 'Now: about Quarles' movements. What can you tell me?'

Frayling made an act of weaving his head. 'You can't expect me to keep tabs on the customers. For one thing I'm too busy running the place.'

'You'd know about meals: who was in, who was out.'

'Not necessarily with guests who are on full board. But I can tell you that Quarles lunched out most days. We packed him baskets to take on the launch.'

'How many is most days?'

'All the week except Friday. Going on the river is why people stay here.'

'Including, say, the Sunday?'

'Not including the Sunday. That day he must have gone out in his car.'

His contact with Rampant, checking of the route.

'Where do the guests make their phone-calls?'

'There's a pay-box down the hall. We switch incoming calls through to it.'

'Did Quarles use it often?'

Frayling shrugged. 'That's something I wouldn't know, isn't it? But he had an incoming call on Friday. I called him down from his room to take it.'

'At what time?'

'Half-past elevenish.'

'Were you around when he took the call?'

'I didn't listen-in, if that's the idea, but I was in the hall talking to the housekeeper. It was a short call, two or three minutes, and the caller was a man with a local accent. Quarles came out of the box looking vexed. He went straight past us up to his room again.'

Rampant, of course.

'You don't remember any calls made?'

'No. But he could have made a dozen.'

'Madame Deslauriers?'

Frayling checked. 'Yes, I saw her in the box once.'

'Which day?'

'The same day, Friday.'

'Friday! Before or after Quarles?'

He puckered his eyes. 'Must have been after. I'd've been going to the dining-room for my pre-lunch inspection.'

'That you can swear to?'

'Yes. Is it important?'

I let my eyes empty. I didn't know. Just that the information touched a nerve which good detectives keep near the surface.

'Where is Madame Deslauriers now?'

'I rather think she's taken a launch out. Incidentally, she's miffed at being made to stay on here. Apparently she has business to see to in London.'

'I'll take that into consideration. Let me see the register.'

Frayling obligingly turned it towards me. During the previous week there had been eighteen other guests and five transients staying at the Barge-House. None of the names meant anything to me. The addresses ranged from Kent to Glasgow. Nearest to Chelsea were a couple called Stanwick who lived in Garden Lane, Chiswick. I shoved the book back.

'Any more to tell me?'

Frayling's eyes jerked, steadied.

'If I remember any more, I'll tell you.'

'Thank you,' I said. 'Please do.'

CHAPTER FIVE

Frayling departed to make apologies to two guests and to prepare their rooms for the gendarmerie. I sought the lounge, a long, sunny room with a view down the lawn to the river. An entertaining place. The two walls facing south and east had been glassed, so that besides the river you could see the bridge, which on this side had its parapet intact. The parapet was of local brick, stone-capped and very elbowable – or would have been, except for the traffic which crashed over the bridge in fractious queues. Rubber-tyred bulldozers, impatient to level it. No more elbows on the comfortable stones. While below blundered other queues, motor-cruisers, battering and scarring brick and stone. Give it two years? Five? They don't really care in these parts. The National Parks Commission turned its back and the joyful exploiters were soon in business.

Several of the late-lunching guests were taking their coffee in the lounge: middle-aged respectables, business-workers, bank-employees, small traders. An atmosphere of defensive politeness, into which

Quarles would probably have merged neatly. With Deslauriers in tow, they would perhaps have put him down as a TV wheel or something in films. Speak nicely, dress well and only a cop can smell your b.o. I took a seat at the back of the house and helped the atmosphere with my pipe.

'Coffee, sir?'

The waiter was intriguing: a long-haired youth with a bush of beard. And a blush.

'Do I know you?'

'N-no, sir. I don't think so.'

But he knew me. Which suggested that Frayling had already briefed his staff.

'What's your name?'

'Bavents, sir.'

It was not a name I would be likely to forget.

'Bring me coffee for two.'

'Yes, sir.'

Dutt arrived as Bavents left.

Dutt was looking pleased. He glanced round the company, then took a seat in my lee.

'I've been having a chat with the landlord, sir. Very interesting it was.'

'Did he have a guest last week?'

'As a matter of fact he had five. But four we don't have to bother with. They were youngsters down here for a bit of sailing.'

'So get to the other one.'

'Yes, sir. He's a lad who registered as Peter Robinson. And he gave an address in Finsbury Park, which I just happen to know doesn't exist.'

'You're sure of that?'

'Dead sure. I go past the place when I drive to work. And this is what makes it really interesting: chummie stayed here for only the one night.'

'Which night?'

'Thursday.'

I clicked my tongue. 'After the snatch, before the kill.'

'Yes, sir. Arrived here during the evening, driving a pale blue Viva. Called himself a speciality salesman and said he might be staying a couple of days. But something must have changed his mind, because he checked out again on Friday morning.'

'What time did he leave?'

'After breakfast.'

'Was he away from the pub at any time during his stay?'

'That evening, sir. He took his bag to his room, went out and didn't return till closing-time.'

'You're right, it is interesting.'

Dutt nodded happily. 'I reckon he could be our killer, sir. A pro they sent up here for the job, some lot who wanted to fix Freddy for good. Just shopping his mob wasn't enough, because Freddy could soon have whipped together a fresh bunch. So they hired this pro. A quiet, out-of-town killing, no strings, no come-back.'

'That's how it could have been.'

'It fits the facts, sir.'

I rasped the bristle on my chin. If that's how it was, then we might as well pack up. The loose ends, if any, were all back in town.

'Did you get a description?'

'A pretty fair one. Aged between thirty and thirty-five. About five-foot-ten, strong build, fair hair with short side-boards, pale eyes. London accent. Wearing a fawn sports jacket with an open-necked shirt and grey slacks.'

'Does it bring anyone to mind?'

'It'd fit Jack Straker.'

'Straker's doing a niner on the Moor.'

'Well, perhaps Fring will talk when they catch him, sir.'

'It's a big perhaps. And they haven't caught him.'

Dutt hunched a little. 'Still, Met may know him. It may give them a lead to the gang who worked it.'

'And that's probably where it will end. In Met's files.' Dutt put on a glum look and stayed silent.

I worked my chin again. 'Just answer me one thing. Is this a job that carries a Straker-type signature?'

'Perhaps not, sir.'

'You know it isn't. There was nothing professional about that knife-attack.'

'But then who is this Peter Robinson joker, sir? Him being here could hardly be a coincidence.'

'The odds are against it. But they're even longer against him being a professional killer. So we'll just hand him on to Hanson and Dainty – and bear him in mind when we're asking questions.'

Dutt looked unconvinced; but Bavents chose that moment to return with the coffee. He poured it with a nervous sort of obsequiousness, his hair weeping round his eyes. Dutt took his cup. I considered Bavents. I was still finding him an intriguing subject.

He draped a napkin round the plated coffee-pot, then referred to his little pad.

'Will that be all, sir?'

'No. Tell me where I should look for Madame Deslauriers.'

'M-Madame Deslauriers?'

'You know her, don't you?'

He was going hot amongst his hair.

'She went out in the l-launch, sir.'

'So I was told. But where do you think she was heading?'

'W-well, you could try the Broad, sir. I heard her asking where she could pick some w-water-lilies.'

I tipped him ten pence. He departed pinkly, doubtless to report to Mr Fr-Frayling. I sipped coffee, then went to the french windows, from which I could see the hotel's boat shed and mooring cut. I saw a runabout moored with three skiffs. I drank up my coffee and returned to Dutt.

'Get off Peter Robinson's description. Then you can make a start with checking statements.'

'Yes, sir,' Dutt said. 'Will you be around?'

I shook my head. 'I'm going on the river.'

The runabout was called *Frolic III*. It was a fibreglass twelve-footer powered by a 20 hp Mercury outboard; it displayed a certain degree of zip as I dodged it downstream among the cruisers. At first, a suicidal-seeming project. The river here was narrow and weltering with craft: clumsy, steep-sided motorised barges that rolled and moaned and crunched their topsides. No effective right and wrong side: just a weak side and a strong side. *Frolic III* was hip, however, and we skated through to less-saturated reaches.

There followed a mile of plugging. I hadn't lost the traffic, but below the village it fell into queues. We grumbled along resignedly between bungalow lawns and saluted moored craft with grinding wash. 200-seater trip-boats thundered by with their 200-sitters waving and jeering. We met one piece of flotsam, a misguided yacht, and left it with its gear bucking and slatting. Then we reached the Broad and the battle of the gateway: when finally the mess could spread out.

I zimmed *Frolic III* across to the reed-beds. I was beginning to wonder if I'd been a fool to come chasing Mimi. The Broad was larger than I had remembered, full of ranging bays and hidden corners. Yachts, allowed a little breeze, loitered across it. I could see numerous launches, moored and manoeuvring. On the opposite bank lay the yacht club, bristling with moorings, where a dozen Mimis might be lurking. I tried to formulate a plan of action that would maximize my chances of meeting her: none occurred to me. I set out to plod conscientiously round the perimeter.

I knew which launch I was looking for because I had asked the boatman at the Barge-House. Mimi had taken the hotel's best boat, *Osprey*, a mahogany, slipper-sterned, twenty-footer. She had left a short while before noon, but had taken no lunch with her; which suggested that either she had stuck among the water-lilies, or had steered for one of the down-river hostelries. Of the latter the nearest was at Harning, about four miles distant. But if she had gone there, then it was likely she would have returned before now. So look out for water-lilies. I pedalled circum-spectly, scanning each inlet for white blossoms.

Twenty minutes later I had reached the south end, where the reeds thinned out into beach-fringed mead-ows. Beyond these, to the west, was a small concealed bay. And in there were the lilies and Mimi's launch.

Mimi wasn't in the launch.

It was moored to a landing-stage that had been built out on piles from the bank. Open water led up to the stage through acres of lilies and their brawling roots. I tinkered *Frolic III* up to the stage; the scent of the lilies was stupefying; alder carrs were hedg-ing them from the modest breeze and they simply lay sunning and disgorging their odours. There was nothing in *Osprey* except her cushions, no sounds but the murmur of distant motors. A still-life of fire-white, saffron-hearted stars, scenting yellow cups, an empty launch and flashing water.

I looped *Frolic III's* painter over a post and climbed out on the stage. A footpath led from it across the meadow and disappeared between high, flowering hawthorn hedges. I followed it. It led to a stile beyond which was a narrow lane. On each side of the lane were fields of green crops, bounded by hedgerows and mature woodlands. Here and there were glimpses of pantile; a long way off stood a sad church-tower. It all basked sleepily in afternoon sunlight and whiffs of fragrance from the hawthorns.

But where was Mimi?

I mounted the stile, intending to continue down the lane. Not necessary. As I straddled the stile, a figure came into view ahead. It had to be Mimi. At a hundred yards range you could feel the vibrations beginning. Seeing me, she hesitated, but then came on. I settled on the stile and waited.

'Madame Deslauriers?'

'Yes, okay?'

The sun wasn't sunnier than the smile she gave me. She had come swinging up to the stile, her bag dangling, and had halted in a playful, swayed stance. Her hair was a warm straw blonde and her eyes a startling emerald green; her features had that majestic, sleeping, symmetry one sometimes finds in Greek marbles.

'Who are you – shall I guess?'

'I'm a policeman.'

'Oh yes, but there are policemen and policemen, huh?'

'My name is Gently. Chief Superintendent.'

'A famous one, yes. That is what I was guessing.'

She dredged up a throaty little laugh. To describe her voice as husky was a simplification. It had an ecstatic, caressing quality that seemed to go straight to the base of your spine.

'You are famous, aren't you?'

'You seem to have heard of me.'

'But no, it is just guessing. Poor Freddy now, he would have heard of you. But the policemen were in his line of business.'

'Is business how you thought of it?'

She made a mouth, and dimpled. 'That's the way it goes, my friend. Cops and robbers. Freddy was a robber. At least you must agree he had talent for it.'

'That didn't help him in the end.'

'No. But I think poor Freddy had got careless. Going out to meet a little rat like Rampant, and at such a place. It wasn't wise.'

'Didn't you try to dissuade him?'

'How could I? Freddy didn't tell me his affairs.'

'Not that Rampant was making trouble?'

Her eyes widened. 'But no! He told me nothing at all. Freddy was a lawyer, you understand? Perhaps that was why he was such a good crook. He told people only what they needed to know, then the policemen can get nothing out of them. And I, what did I need to know? I am just his woman, that's all. He would say, It has been a good week, we have cleared so-and-so, you can read about it in this paper. Okay?'

'And you didn't want to know more?'

'Ha, ha. Why should I be interested in crookery? Do you think I am a crook?'

'You have been associating with one.'

'No, Monsieur. Just with a man.'

Well, it was believable. I eyed her clinically. Not only the face was borrowed from Praxiteles. With a body as regal as that one might not feel the need for additional excitements.

'Were you fond of Quarles?'

She swirled her hair. 'He was a man of great *savoir faire*, Freddy. He could talk about this, about that. It did not matter what company he was in.'

'But you were fond of him.'

'He was fun to be with.'

'That isn't really answering the question.'

She warmed her smile for me. 'Perhaps I don't like

the question. So perhaps I'm not going to give you an answer.'

'Then I'll draw my own conclusion. You weren't fond of him.'

She pouted prettily. 'Perhaps, I said. Maybe I don't know myself, exactly. That sometimes happens to one, huh?'

'At least, you're not grief-stricken.'

'I am sad, oh yes. After all, we had been together three years. But grief-stricken, no. I have had one big grief, and after that—' She gestured. 'So say I am sad.'

'Or even less than that?'

Her eyes narrowed slightly. Then she thrust her bag at me.

'Here – hold this! It is time I permitted myself a cigarette.'

Which brought us closer: I sitting on the stile, Mimi extracting a cigarette from the bag I was holding. Then, strangely, she couldn't find her matches, had to beg a light from me: and steady my hand. Fingers of character. Not anonymously feminine, but made to do something more than caress. And I caught that scent which Hanson had likened to honey, and which I immediately qualified: heather honey.

'I am told you wish to go back to London.'

'Oh, perhaps. It is not important.'

'Some business was mentioned.'

'Not true. Just some parties, a first night.'

'Then you won't mind staying here a little longer.'

She blew me a tender stream of smoke. 'No. It will not be so boring. It is the small men I find tiresome.'

'After all, you seem able to amuse yourself.'

'Aha. So you have noticed.'

'Picking water-lilies. Where did you put them?'

'They have horrible stems, my friend. No good.'

'Yet you found them so intriguing that they made you miss lunch.'

'Is that why my tummy feels empty?'

'Did you miss lunch?'

She blew smoke pettishly. 'This is a foolish conversation.'

'But did you miss it?'

She took the bag. 'I must have done. I am suddenly bored. So now I go straight back to have a meal. Au r'voir, my friend. Enjoy the daisies.'

CHAPTER SIX

Sᴴᴇ ᴍᴏᴜɴᴛᴇᴅ ᴛʜᴇ stile with quick grace and jumped down lightly into the meadow.

'Wait,' I said.

'Why should I wait?'

'I have some more questions to ask you.'

She slitted her eyes. 'And if I am not in the mood? If I do not choose to be pestered?'

I shook my head. 'You are too intelligent. You would never take up a foolish attitude.'

'Foof!' But her mouth twitched. 'You know that you have no right to detain me. And I am not very pleased to be harassed like this, to be chased by a policeman when I stretch my legs.'

'Is that what you were doing?'

'Of course. Do you doubt it?'

'I don't doubt you could find a way to be more helpful.'

'Huh-huh. And why should I?'

'Because it would amuse you. And I make a change from the clientele at the Barge-House.'

She drew herself up. 'Monsieur, what vanity!'

'Also, you're not yet sure if I admire you.'

She gave a throbbing chuckle. 'I think you are a devil. What a good thing I find you unattractive.'

We stared at each other. She was smiling now.

'Okay, okay, we will play the game. I find I am not hungry after all. It must be the scent of so many flowers.'

'Shall we go back to the launch?'

'I prefer not. It will be more comfortable out of the sun.' She glanced around casually. 'Perhaps beneath that hawthorn. It seems unlikely that we shall be disturbed.'

She stubbed her cigarette and made for the hawthorn. It was the most spreading of several that fringed the meadow; a handsome pyramid of milky blossom, throwing broken shade on the grass beneath. Mimi selected her spot and sat down; I selected mine, leaving turf between us. From there you saw a steely slice of the Broad with distant sails moving slowly upon it. Mimi plucked a stalk of plantain and chewed it appreciatively. She had turned towards me and was leaning on her elbow. Two harnessless breasts were moulding themselves sweetly, one drooping, one pouted by its neighbour.

'Are you married, my friend?'

'Not entirely.'

'Hah. Such wisdom in two words. Is she so beautiful?'

'I don't carry her photograph.'

'Then she is either very beautiful or very plain. I wonder which.'

I let her wonder. 'How did you come to take up with Quarles?'

55

'Oh, I was unhappy. It was after my trouble. Two million Frenchmen wanted to marry me.'

'And you didn't want to marry?'

She bit off some stalk. 'I am rich too, that is the trouble. My late husband was an industrialist. If he had been poor there would have been no trial. La Famille. His poisonous mother. No doubt you are provided with the details. Afterwards, who cares about marrying Mimi? The bride is so many million francs.'

'And Quarles was so different?'

'Oh, but yes. I think you do not understand. Freddy also was rich, very rich. It is all tucked away in a little Swiss bank. So what did Freddy care about marrying rich girls? No, my friend, this was love. He picked me up one night in Montparnasse. He was a thief. I let him steal me.'

'Did you know he was a thief?'

'Not that first night. But he didn't know I was a rich girl, either. Then it was too late. We make these grand discoveries when it would be disagreeable to let them interfere. So, we ignore them. He doesn't want my money, nor do I wish to reform Freddy. After all, he is brilliant in his line. What chance has he ever given you to catch him?'

'Somebody did catch him.'

'Aha. But that somebody was not a policeman. In the end perhaps he catches himself. Or it is just that the little crooks grow envious.'

'Which little crooks?'

'Why not Rampant?'

'It wasn't Rampant who tipped the police.'

'No, you are sure?'

I popped the head of a daisy. 'So if not Rampant, who would it be?'

She drew her stalk through her teeth. 'Well, it wasn't me. I had no reason to shop Freddy. Was it a woman's voice?'

'That's not important. It wouldn't exclude a woman's having been behind it.'

'Ah, ah, it was a man, then. The rest is guessing. You are just trying it on, my friend. I think you had better stick to this little pig, Rampant. Because, after all, who is going to believe him?'

She elevated a knee, and admired it. The action slid her hem down her thigh. She had a strong, distinctive leg that flowered from an athletic foot and ankle. She smiled and let the knee slowly unflex: leaving the hem where it was.

'You think I was tired of Freddy, huh?'

'Were you ever really in love with him?'

She made a small mouth. 'I think so, at first. Those first few weeks were formidable. It was like bubbles up my nose, I could scarcely get my breath. Better than my husband, oh yes. It is a shame to kill a man like Freddy.'

'But you were through with him by Friday.'

'You are right.' She sighed. 'So then it may not really have been love. I am swept off my feet, as you say. Freddy took me on the bounce. But still I am fond of him, huh? He was such an interesting man to live with. Such a wide acquaintance. They knew he was a crook, but it didn't matter. He was always welcome.'

'He was jealous of you.'

She gave her gurgling chuckle. 'All men are jeal-ous, more or less.'

'Perhaps you'd given him cause.'

'But why not? We are only young for you once, my friend.'

'Then he resented it.'

'And I killed him?'

'Well?'

She rolled on her stomach and squirmed closer to me. 'No.' It was spoken as though to a child. 'You are trying so hard, petit. So hard.'

I thrummed another daisy-head at the meadow. Mimi picked daisies and thrummed one, too. Hers landed squarely on my chin. She giggled and lined up another. Two bull's-eyes. I shifted further off; Mimi squirmed after me like a seal. She rested her chin in her hands and stared up at me, her breasts pendant among the daisies.

'Forget it,' she said. 'I didn't kill him. Even though he was so stupidly jealous. Even though he threatened me with violence. There he was weak. And he knew I knew it.'

'And you, of course, weren't jealous of him.'

'Shall I tell you the truth?'

'If it isn't being old-fashioned.'

'Yes, I was jealous. Isn't that strange? I couldn't bear him eyeing another woman.'

'Which sometimes he did?'

She nodded. 'Sometimes. And that made me so angry. Perhaps I am thinking I am much the most beautiful, so why does he insult me like that, huh?'

'Was there any particular woman?'

'Oh no. I would have left him on the spot.'

'Please think carefully. It could be important.'

'I tell you for certain. No particular woman.'

'Just you.'

'Wouldn't you say I was enough? I never grew stale with poor Freddy. And I didn't need to kill him, that's certain too: if I had grown tired of him, I could have left.' She let fly with a daisy. 'So you had better believe me, instead of thinking up such useless questions.'

'I believe anything I can prove.'

'Oh, foof.' She plucked and loaded a fresh daisy.

I grabbed her firing-hand. She liked that, and let the daisy fall to the grass. The hand had a cool, consenting feel; it moved lazily under mine. But I dropped it. She lay still, leaving the hand where it fell.

'Tell me about your stay here.'

'Must you waste our time, my friend?'

'Did you know that Freddy had come on a job?'

She sighed expressively. 'He didn't tell me.'

'But you knew?'

'Okay, I knew. Freddy would not have come here just for pleasure. A bourgeois inn wasn't his style. It isn't my style, either.'

'How did he propose it?'

'Oh, very politely. He is thinking we would like a week out of town.'

'It didn't arise from some . . . earlier circumstance?'

She stared. 'Of course, he had the tip from Rampant.'

'But nothing else?'

'What should there be?'

I shrugged. 'The Bryanston job wasn't a grand one. I would like to know why Freddy bothered with it. Whether there was something else in the wind.'

She gazed for a while. 'You are subtle,' she said. 'This is why they make you top man.'

'Have you any suggestions?'

'None, my friend. Unless it is that this Rampant misleads Freddy.'

I shook my head. 'Freddy was a specialist. He could cost a job like an accountant. He would have checked the size of the Bryanston labour-force and multiplied it by the average wage-rate. Add a percentage for over-time and N.H.I., deduct a percentage for the sick and absent. The result would give him a minimum figure, probably accurate within a few thousands.'

'Freddy did all that?'

'On his cuff. He'd know exactly what he was going for.'

She giggled. 'I think I'm proud of Freddy. I think he really was a clever man.'

'Not so clever with this job, though.'

'Perhaps he does it just to show his skill.'

'You can't help me.'

'I am so sorry.'

'Right. Now let's talk about Peter Robinson.'

Her eyes widened; were suddenly empty.

'Why should we talk about a shop?'

'Not the shop. A man. A man who was at Haughton Thursday evening.'

'But I do not know any Peter Robinson.'

'A man of about your own age. Five-foot-ten, fair hair with sideboards, comes from town, drives a blue Viva.'

'But no, I don't know him.'

'He spent the night at the Three Tuns.'

'I have never visited that place.'

'He was out during the evening. Perhaps paying a call.'

'I cannot help it – I didn't see him!'

I paused, holding her eyes. 'Where were you Thursday evening?'

Now she was sitting up straight in the grass. 'In the hotel, of course – at first on the lawn—'

'With Quarles?'

'Yes! Why should I not say true?'

'And after that?'

'Then we go into dinner – and in the bar – and watch TV—'

'Still with Quarles?'

'Of course! With Freddy.'

'Until you went to bed, never alone?'

She drew quick breaths, her eyes glinting. Her hands were clasping her flexed knees. I had her going; but suddenly she realized it: suddenly let the tension go. She gave a breathless chuckle.

'Ha-ha! You are trying to bulldoze me, huh?'

'Were you alone?'

'You are fierce, my friend. I adore a man with a touch of steel.'

'Please answer the question.'

'I grow so weak. A man like that can do what he

wants with me. I melt for him, huh? A couple of times I go to the loo.'

'Twice?'

'It may be three times. Why do you bore me with such nonsense?'

'Then you could have been available for a brief interview.'

'I prefer the longer ones. All night.'

I gave it up. She'd turned on her back, with a knee crooked and waving. Her arms were folded behind her head, her eyes thinned, lips parted. Venus inviting. And I couldn't be certain if she was covering-up or not.

'Have you been to this part of England before?'

'I am a Parisienne, Monsieur.'

'Meaning yes, or no?'

'Would that be likely? I have not even heard of it before this time.'

'Then you have no friends here?'

'None.'

'Nobody to speak to on the phone.'

She hesitated. 'Now you ask something different. It is not only to friends that one speaks on the phone.'

'Then who was it on Friday?'

She re-composed her legs; crooking both knees, letting them spread.

'Don't you want to answer?'

'Just thinking, Monsieur. Let us say it was Friday when I phoned the theatre.'

'The theatre!'

'But yes. They have a theatre in the town. One day

I feel desolate, think it will amuse me. Perhaps Friday, I do not know.'

'Only, of course, there were no suitable seats.'

Her lips twitched. 'Monsieur knows.'

'And you gave no name, so they wouldn't remember you.'

She released a hand to make a gesture.

'And I am supposed to believe this.'

She came coiling across to me. 'Monsieur will believe what he likes, won't he?' She hung on my shoulder. 'But it doesn't matter. Because perhaps it was another day, after all.'

'Though having no connection with Peter Robinson.'

'Aha! I think that man makes you jealous. But there is no need, my fierce friend. I can truthfully say I have not met him.'

'Not then or later.'

'Not at all.'

'Not, for example, today at lunch.'

I felt her tense: the weight of flesh grew a little less on my arm.

'Now I think you are teasing me.'

'Really? How long has your launch been moored over there?'

'One hour, two. How would I know? I am beginning to feel it is too long.'

'Where does the lane lead?'

'You must ask a map.' She broke from me quickly and got to her feet. 'This talk of lunch makes me hungry again, Monsieur. It is sad, but I fear our game is over.'

I didn't budge. 'Au r'voir, Madame.'

She paused to give me a sharp stare. Then she tossed her hair with superb disdain and set off for the staithe. She didn't look back.

CHAPTER SEVEN

THE LAUNCH LEFT; I watched it make its turn and go creaming away up the Broad; then I sat beneath the hawthorn a few minutes longer, moodily sorting out my results.

They were not encouraging.

In the first place, I couldn't link Peter Robinson to the crime. He had turned up *a propos*, giving a false name and address, but otherwise he wasn't implicated. True, I had made a pass with him at Madame Deslauriers and seemed to have got a small bite; but it was a very small one, and the reaction may not have been due to Peter Robinson.

Bringing me to the second place. If Madame Deslauriers had a secret, it didn't necessarily link with the crime either. In fact it probably didn't, because she had no motive: Quarles had been no obstruction to her. Her secret, if she had one, was probably a lover whom she felt it injudicious to produce at this moment: whether Peter Robinson or another villain who might come gratefully to our hand.

All very semi-innocent. And yet . . .

I rose and went back to stare at the lane.

It was such an *excessively* discreet place for a rendezvous. You would almost say it would be wasted on a pair of lovers.

I got over the stile and continued to the bend. Beyond it the lane entered a plantation; then it stretched away between ranks of wild parsley to meet a minor road a quarter of a mile distant. The surface was dried, rutted mud, and the straggling parsley suggested little use. But here and there a frond was broken, and the damaged leafage had not yet shrivelled. A car? A car must have turned. The only place for that would be the plantation. I checked back till I found a gap between trees, then the plain marks of wheels in grassed leaf-mould. I followed them. They entered the plantation; stopped and criss-crossed in a little clearing. Here the car had parked, out of sight from the lane, the precise spot shown by the deeper indentations. I prowled around. Cores, apple-peelings; screwed-up wrappings from chocolate biscuits. Fresh: the peel hadn't browned, the wrappings had taken no damp from the ground. The car-tracks were unidentifiable, but the car had not been a large one, credibly a Viva. And along with the tracks were a number of footprints: these similarly unidentifiable.

So what more had I now?

A small matter of confirmation: that Mimi was in contact with a person unknown; and whom she wanted to keep unknown.

And whom she was probably dashing back to warn by phone.

★   ★   ★

I handed in the runabout, collected the Lotus and drove through rush-hour traffic to Norchester. I found Hanson in his office; he was drinking beer and eating fish-and-chips from a newspaper package. I went over my facts. Hanson listened, scowling.

'That lane would be Sallowes way,' he said. 'Are you saying there's a chummie hiding out there?'

'It's a possibility. And he could be the man who stayed at the Three Tuns on Thursday.'

'You think he's the killer?'

'We don't know that. We do know he's in contact with Deslauriers.'

Hanson worried a chip. 'I still fancy Rampant. I wish I could believe he's a brilliant liar.'

He fetched a map and we found the lane. It connected with a back road between Sallowes and Wrackstead. By water about two miles from Haughton, by road nearer seven, when you knew the way. In the vicinity were two farms and a scattered handful of farm cottages; Sallowes village was two miles one way, Wrackstead village four miles in the other.

'Is there a pub at Sallowes?'

'Yeah, The Peal of Bells.'

Hanson reached for the phone and talked to the switchboard. Two minutes later he was connected; they had had no guests at The Peal of Bells.

'Any guest-houses? Private lodgings?'

'There's nothing of that sort at Sallowes. A bit of housing development, mostly commuters. Perhaps chummie is camping in a field.'

'He'll be close to a telephone.'

'Well, that should help. I'll ask the County to do

some checking. Only if he isn't the chummie with the blue Viva, how are we going to know him when we find him?'

A good question.

'He'll have been around since Friday, possibly all the preceding week. A man on his own, no apparent business. Most likely from London or that direction.'

Hanson hefted a shoulder. 'So we'll look. But it could be Timmy from Timbuctoo.' He ate a few chips. 'Meanwhile there's Rampant. You haven't got closer than him yet.'

I used Hanson's phone to ring Dainty. Dainty had a tale of woe to tell. He had just missed laying hands on Fring at the staked-out house in Battersea. At about 2 p.m. a Ford Zephyr came by with a driver resembling Fring. It had slowed, pulled in, then departed in haste, the driver obviously having smelled a rat. Alarms and excursions. They had found the Zephyr (it was stolen) across the river in Chelsea, but no Fring, no money; and now the stake-out had been blown.

I made sympathetic noises. 'What about our Peter Robinson?'

Dainty sounded less than interested. 'You have to admit your description is vague.' I was getting that reaction from everywhere.

'This chummie has been missing from his usual haunts.'

'So have half the chummies we know.'

'The description would fit someone like Jack Straker.'

'Straker's away. Hadn't you heard?'

I passed on my little bit of information about

Quarles' deposits in a Swiss bank. That didn't cheer Dainty either: but I hadn't supposed it would. He came back with something else.

'We found Quarles' will in his safe deposit.'

'He left a will?'

'It's dated last August. It leaves his whole estate to Mimi Deslauriers.'

I chewed that over as I drove back to Haughton. It had a chilling sort of ring to it. By her own account, Mimi was a rich woman, but her account was all I had. And even if it were true, this was motive. The rich are not averse to becoming richer. Nor must I forget that previous occasion when a man had died to Mimi's profit.

A second shake with the same dice?

But that would mean she had known about the will. Quarles, ex-lawyer, master-criminal, would surely have kept his counsel in a matter so sensitive. And supposing she had known: then I had still to construe the crime as a plot devised by her, whereas the principal circumstances were arranged by Quarles, and the murder apparently a piece of opportunism. To make it credible, one would have to assume communication and conspiracy between her and Rampant: not to mention the shadowy Peter Robinson, necessary if Rampant jibbed at the killing. Possible, but highly unlikely: it would have left her at the mercy of two con-federates. Mimi was much too *au fait* for that. A simple jostle at a tube station would have served her better.

And yet . . . Quarles must have been worth a great deal of money.

If it hadn't been Mimi, then perhaps a secondary operator?

For example, Peter Robinson, with a hold on Mimi, working through her to net Freddy's jackpot . . . ?

I shook my head: this was thinking like Hanson – trying to angle it away from Mimi! Mimi, who had no need to murder anyone, who could do it all with the drop of a bra. Not practical thinking. Mimi could kill, perhaps had blood on her hands already. The field was open.

And now I knew of one lode-stone that could have applied a fatal deflection.

I parked in the yard at the Barge-House and went in to confer with Dutt. Dutt was refreshing himself in the lounge, where Mimi, with a group of admirers, was also installed. She favoured me with a vivacious wave and a cooing 'Hallo!' – which I acknowledged with a dead-bat nod; her appetite, officially unlunched, appeared to have been satisfied with toast and jam.

I joined Dutt, who was sitting alone and looking every inch a copper. A waiter, not Bavents, came up and took my order for tea and toast.

Dutt nodded towards Mimi. 'I see you clicked, sir.'

I grunted. 'And what have you been up to?'

Dutt looked sly. 'There's a little maid called Nancy. We spent quite a time going over her statement.'

'And what did you get – in the way of business?'

'In the way of business, not very much, sir. But the head-waiter, Colby, remembered something.'

'Save him till after I've had my cuppa.'

I drank and ate, while up the lounge Mimi continued to glamorize the peasants. She was clever with it: she talked to the wives and left the husbands to drink her in. She had changed out of the shortie dress she'd been wearing and put on a clinging gown with a split skirt. Most of one clamorous leg was on view, and though the bust was now harnessed, it was cleft to infinity.

'She does fetch them in, sir,' Dutt murmured wistfully.

I crunched some toast. 'You keep your heart for Nancy.'

'Yes, sir. But you can't help admiring it. I reckon you admire the mostest in anything.'

I finished, and lit my unromantic pipe. 'Now, if we can, let's get back to Colby.'

Dutt sighed and dragged his eyes away. He cleared his throat, trying to sound like business.

'Colby is the big, bald-headed man, sir. I got him remembering about last Thursday. How the deceased and the lady went out in a launch with a couple called Silverman, man and wife. They came back again about four-ish and sat in the lounge, like now. Then, after dinner, Colby went for a drink and remained in the bar for half-an-hour. He says Quarles was in there along with the Silvermans, but he doesn't recall seeing the lady.'

'He could scarcely have overlooked her.'

'It seems the bar was pretty full, sir. Colby was sitting with a mate in a corner.'

'And everyone else would have been sitting round Mimi.'

'So there it is, sir. She was missing.'

But missing where?

'What time was this?'

'Colby says from nine till half-past.'

'Did anyone else see her during that time?'

'Nobody I've had a talk with yet, sir.'

I puffed expansively. It was fitting all right. At eight Peter Robinson had arrived at the Three Tuns. Had booked in and gone out, say at eight-thirty. Half-an-hour to contact Mimi. How had he done it?

'Are any of the staff very friendly with the lady?'

'Reckon all of them are, sir. The men especially.'

'These young waiters. Is there one with a crush?'

Dutt looked blank. 'As much one as another, sir. Though I did hear of one she sort of makes use of, gets to run errands, fetch things to her room.'

'Who?'

'The Bavents kid, sir. But he was off this afternoon. I haven't talked to him yet.'

Dutt was using the reception office for interrogation, and there I had Bavents brought when he returned. He was looking even furrier in a T-shirt and jeans: like a narrow-faced Jesus fresh back from the wilderness. I pointed to a chair and he sat nervously. I had his statement to Hanson on the desk before me.

'You are Adam Bavents?'

'That's me.'

'I see it says here that you are a student.'

Bavents flicked back a lock from his nose. 'I told the other man all about that.'

72

'Now tell me.'

'So that's w-what I am, then. A third-year student at Norchester U.'

'If you are a student, what are you doing here?'

'I'm just filling in time till next term.'

Oh yes. 'And why is that?'

He jerked a look over his shoulder. 'I got sent down. It isn't a secret. They said I was ring-leader of a demo.'

'And were you?'

'I might have been. I'm not ashamed of it. They were trying to sack a tutor for speaking out against racialism.'

'Wasn't that when the students smashed up a lecture-hall?'

He stared through his hair. 'We had to make our point.'

'But by violence.'

'If you call that violence.'

I nodded. 'Yes, I call that violence. And violence is what I have come here about. So I seem to have reached the right quarter.'

His tresses rustled. 'But that's just talk! I don't know anything about the other.'

'But about anti-racialism you know something. Tell me, what are your feelings towards the French?'

A sweaty silence. His hair fondled the T-shirt, showed his nose through a Gothic window. A pink nose: and pink hands rucking the fade-spots in his jeans. Then his mouth loosened.

'I didn't kill him!'

'Fine. What happened on Thursday evening?'

'Th-Thursday?'

73

'In the evening. When the men wanted a word with Madame Deslauriers.'

'I – I—'

'Where were you that evening?'

'I – I was w-working on my car!'

'You have a car?'

'Yes! A Mini—'

'And you were working on it – in the yard?'

'Yes, but—'

'You were handy then. Handy for this man coming into the yard. Who wanted a message slipped to Madame Deslauriers. Fair hair, sideboards. What name did he give?'

'He d-didn't – I wasn't—'

'Oh come on, now. He was staying at the Tuns. Did you know that?'

'I tell you—'

'Drives a blue Viva. Come on, the name's on the tip of your tongue.'

'But I s-swear—'

'You say you didn't kill Quarles?'

'No! I don't know anything about it!'

'So then let's have the name of this man.'

He went into a huddle with his hair.

'Listen,' I said. 'You've let something slip. Now I know you ran the message for that man. And if you get nicked on a conspiracy charge you'll be filling in time for longer than a term. So you'd better talk while you still have the chance.'

'I d-don't have anything to tell you.'

'Because you love Madame so much?'

'That isn't t-true!'

'I'll remember to ask her.'

He jumped up from his chair.

'Hold it,' I said. 'Is this your signature on the statement?'

'Of course it's m–my signature!'

'That surprises me. Just do a specimen underneath.'

His eyes sparkled through his mane, baffled. Then he grabbed a pen from the desk and jerked off a signature. The same, of course, less a margin for nerves. He slammed down the pen in feeble triumph.

'Now may I go?'

'For the present.'

He towed his hair out of the office. Dutt, a silent spectator, gave me a wink. I fanned myself with the twice-signed statement.

'An interesting customer.'

'Yes, sir. I'd say that ties in our Peter Robinson.'

'There's something else.'

'The signature, sir?'

I shook my head. 'He's left-handed.'

CHAPTER EIGHT

Left-handed; but so is every tenth person, according to a reliable set of statistics; and adding it together, there didn't seem much ground for placing Bavents on the list of suspects. He might have loved Mimi and loathed Quarles, but that scarcely qualified as a live motive. He had no prospect of stepping into Quarles' shoes, and without such bait his interest was marginal.

Or did he have a prospect. . .?

I played with the thought, giving it a chance to attract credibility; trying to visualize his hairy highness as a demon lover for whom Mimi would be content to risk her all. But it wouldn't focus. Mimi was too sophisticated. She had too much emotional poise. She might give him a tumble for the novelty of it, but that would be the summit for Master Bavents. The Quarleses were her taste, suave and tough: men who didn't know how to stutter. The rest were to run and serve: lackeys and go-betweens: Baventses.

Which didn't mean I had lost interest in Bavents, who certainly hadn't told us all he knew; or that it would be unprofitable to probe there a little, seeking out a perhaps-unsuspected conjunction.

I met Frayling in the hall and invited him into the office.

'How did you come to employ Adam Bavents?'

Frayling flickered me his harassed, ingratiating smile: a promise of satisfaction in exchange for modest patience.

'He applied for the job. I'm always short of waiters.'

'How did he know the job was vacant?'

'Oh, they run an employment section in the students' magazine. It lists details of jobs going in the vacations.'

'You knew why he was sent down?'

'Of course. I asked him. But things like that don't count much these days. He seemed a decent sort of youngster, and I haven't had any complaints.'

'What are his hours?'

'Seven to eight-thirty. Two afternoons and one evening off.

'Which evening?'

'The evening varies.'

'Which was it last week?'

Frayling wriggled. 'Friday.'

One conjunction.

'Would you know if he went out?'

Frayling's smile became more harassed. 'I imagine he did, that's what one would expect. But he might well have been studying in his room.'

'Where's his room?'

'It's off the back landing. A room we keep free for temporary staff.'

'How close to Madame Deslauriers' room?'

Well . . . next-door, I suppose! But a door shuts-off the landing.'

Two conjunctions?

'Isn't Bavents Madame's favourite?'

'No, really! That's putting it too strong. He serves at her table, that's all. Guests tend to adopt their regular waiter.'

'But something of that sort?'

'No, I protest. You must have been listening to staff gossip.'

'Wouldn't the staff know?'

But Frayling still protested, so I let him go to get on with ushering dinner.

At dinner I had an opportunity of studying Madame and her waiter together. Mimi had one of the best tables, with a view of the river: rather remote from our late-comer's corner. She sat alone, but this didn't prevent her from conversing merrily with her nearest neighbours. Bavents came, went, and did his duty: if anything special passed, I failed to notice it. Had Frayling cautioned him? More than likely. But Frayling could scarcely have cautioned Mimi. Mimi must have taken her own counsel to preserve distance, a circumstance not without significance.

Once or twice she glanced at our table, but each time managed to avoid my eye. Then she would eat silently for a few moments before engaging in some fresh sally with the neighbours. She was as conscious of me as I of her; her rattle of small talk was a screen; through the subdued busyness of the peopled room a strand of tension stretched between us. Excellent: it gave me appetite. Madame was not so confident after all. I had begun to tread a little on her skirt, might have set it fraying at the edges.

Beside me Dutt ate ploddingly and well, though not without his own eye for the lady. He nudged me once:

'Do you reckon it's all natural?'

'Get on with your dinner.'

He chortled into his trifle.

We had coffee on the lawn, from where we could watch late motor-cruisers raising wash over the quay-headings. While we drank I pondered the utility of tackling Mimi then or of letting her sleep on it. On the whole I favoured the latter (it had been a long day); so I went in to ring Brenda: who for the second time surprised me with quite unpredictable information.

'George. I've been talking to Siggy about your corpse.'

'Thank you. But it's still eating hot dinners.'

'Not that one, idiot! Flash Freddy. Did you know he was going to retire?'

'Retire?'

'That's what I said. He'd been talking of giving up business. He'd bought a villa in the South of France, Cap Ferrat way. Hadn't you heard?'

'No, I hadn't heard.'

'Well, it's true, because Siggy borrowed it for a week last summer. He says it's a super place, perched on a cliff, with a private beach and all the etceteras.'

'How nice for Siggy. He knows nice people.'

'George, I think you ought to be grateful. If one of your relatives is chummy with crooks, the least you can do is to profit by it.'

I grunted. John Sigismund Fazakerly is a relative only by marriage. My first act on meeting him was to arrest him, which doesn't make him my favourite in-law.

'What was the retiring bit?'

'Just what I said. Siggy and he were chatting about Riviera properties. About Somerset Maugham, the English set. Freddy said soon, he was going to retire there.'

'Did he mention a date?'

'Stupid. He just said he was getting bored with business. I suppose it can happen to crooks like every-one else. The day comes when it doesn't switch them on. He was rich enough, wasn't he?'

'Oh quite.'

'There you are, then. He wanted to relax. If some imbecile hadn't gone sticking a knife in him, Freddy would soon have been out of your hair.'

A comforting thought.

'Only it isn't quite like that. Crooks don't find it so easy to retire.'

'Why not?'

'They tend to have disapproving associates – men who can make their point with a knife.'

'Hah.' She was silent for a moment. 'Are you saying that's what happened to Freddy?'

'I wish I knew. But what you've told me does sug-gest the possibility.'

A further silence. 'That's disappointing.'

'Why?'

'Because I've got a bet on with Siggy. A fiver on Mimi Deslauriers' nose. Siggy's fiver is on Rampant.'

'You could both be wrong.'

'Not me. Never. Don't you remember my intuition?'

'Not as a viable force.'

'Nuts to you. Just remember to keep your eye on Mimi.'

Followed a slightly more pregnant silence.

'How are you doing with her?'

'You could say we understand each other.'

'Pig! Is she making a play for you?'

'That wouldn't single me out in a crowd.'

Brenda made ferocious noises. 'You listen, George Gently! That woman'll be poison if she gets you to bed with her. She'll have you doing somersaults to keep her out of it. And then bang will go my fiver.'

'Why make these rash bets?'

'Do you hear me talking to you? Just take a tip from someone who knows.'

'I'll keep it in mind when the lights go out. What else did Siggy have to tell you?'

Brenda fumed again. 'I'm not sure I'll tell you. I wouldn't if I thought it was at all important. It's just that Freddy mentioned some other properties he owned, two in Scotland and one on the Broads.'

'What!'

'You needn't get excited. He didn't tell Siggy where they were. I expect they're little bolt-holes where he could lie low when people like you were being unfriendly.'

'Was there any description?'

'No, there wasn't. Only exactly what I've told you.'

'A cottage – bungalow?'

'Three properties. Think about that when the lights go out.'

I got from her the address of the Cap Ferrat villa, then sat for a while, my hand on the phone. But first things first. I rang H.Q., who gave me Hanson's private number.

'Any progress re Peter Robinson?'

'Hell, I'm watching a programme,' Hanson said indignantly. 'There's nothing in.'

'Then listen to this. I've had a tip that Quarles owned property on the Broads.'

'What sort of property?'

'That's the bonus question. But it will be one only occasionally inhabited. Owned by a Londoner, sure to have a phone, probably in a remote situation.'

'But the Broads are lousy with properties like that. Three parts of the bungalows are owned by foreigners.'

'This one will have Peter Robinson living in it. And a blue Viva in the garage.'

'You reckon so?'

'Look at the facts. He booked in at the Three Tuns for an indefinite stay. Then he made contact with Deslauriers, that's been established, and checked out of the Three Tuns, but remained in the district. So where else?'

'You think she hid him there?'

'Can you suggest a better prospect? If the hideaway was good enough for Quarles, then it would surely be good enough for Peter Robinson.'

'So then maybe it'll take a bit of finding.'

'We have one fix. It's handy for Sallowes. That suggests it's on the south side of the river, because Haughton's the only crossing for miles.'

'That still leaves it open. It could be on the South River.'

'Either way, we have to find it. I want County to treat this as a matter of urgency. Picking up Robinson is top priority.'

'You want immediate action.'

'I want that.'

I heard Hanson sigh. 'Will do.'

Then I rang London, where after a ten-minute delay they connected me with Dainty. Similarities in background noise suggested he had been occupied in the same way as Hanson. I told him about Quarles' villa, about Quarles' talk of retiring.

'Who do we know who would take that to heart?'

Dainty hedged. 'I could name you a dozen. Quarles has master-minded for several of the gangs as well as running his own mob. He could put away some top villains and none of them would stop at having him done.'

'But you can narrow that down.'

'Do you think I haven't been trying? I've had whispers about O'Leary and Whitey Ferrier. I have men out now trying to get the dope on them. We haven't been sitting on our hands all day.'

'Have you had another session with Quarles' boys?'

'Don't make me laugh. They've clammed solid.'

'You could let it out that Fring was playing them double, was hooked in with other interests.'

'It's been tried. They were there. They're not going to believe that Fring planned his skarper.'

'A few days in the cells would give them time to wonder.'

'Have it your way. But they haven't talked yet.'

I shrugged to myself. 'Let's get to Fring, then. How sure was the identification today?'

Dainty hesitated. 'Are you questioning that?'

'I'm thinking you won't be the only ones looking for him. The story has been blown for two days. A man on the loose with thirty-five grand. Fring might have come cruising by his house today, but so might some other interested parties.'

'Sergeant Dymock thought it was Fring.'

'Has Dyrnock met him?'

'He's studied photographs.'

'Then there's room for error. Fring may be still with us, or he may be catching a tan on a private beach.'

I heard Dainty suck breath. 'Quarles' villa?'

'It's only a short flight from Heathrow. And today's was your only sighting of Fring. Unless you're positive, I'd say he's skipped.'

'You could be right. We've had no whispers.'

'Which could also mean he's floating down the Thames.'

'I like the first idea best. You'd better give me particulars of the villa.'

I dictated them, against background music and a voice that sounded like Harry Corbett's.

'Fine,' Dainty said. 'I'll ring Interpol. How are things shaping at your end?'

'Packed with psychological interest.'

He gave a dirty laugh. 'I've heard about her. When do you get to the ooh la la?'

I hung up: but sat a little longer, very silent, on the padded desk-chair. From across the hall was coming the murmur of the bar, but that wasn't the only sound I had been hearing. Now I rose quietly and moved to the door. Nothing to see through the glass panels. I whipped open the door and stepped out. Bavents was pressed against the wall alongside.

'Were you able to hear, then?'

He started away from me, but I was blocking his retreat down the hall. He stood frightened-eyed, breathing quickly, looking oddly Victorian in his waiter's tails.

'I – I wasn't listening!'

'Pull the other one.'

'I was w-waiting to use the phone.'

'What's wrong with the call-box?'

'I don't have any change!'

'But you do get free use of the office phone?'

Bavents was trembling. Just then, however, some people came out of the bar behind him. I had to make way for them, way for Bavents. He grabbed the opportunity and went.

Not that it mattered. As Joe Louis once said, they can run but they can't hide.

CHAPTER NINE

BUT THIS INCIDENT settled one thing: my session with Mimi could not now wait till morning. I didn't know whether or not she had set Bavents to spy on me, but there was a strong possibility that she would get his report. I went into the bar. Drinkers were grouped round the piano, at which someone sat playing *La Mer*. I pushed up till I could see the pianist: it was Mimi, of course: her Parisian thing. She was playing *La Mer* with a languorous unction and no mean skill in the fingering, evoking, with poised, resonant octaves, an American's idea of the mood of the boulevards. It was musical ham, but being played with a conviction that stripped the tinsel from the cliché. And the group of drinkers hummed it with her, swaying slowly to the wave-like rhythm.

I eased my way to the piano and found a corner on which to lean my elbow. Mimi's eyes connected with mine: she hooded them provocatively and leaned towards me. She began singing in French. Her hoarse contralto was thrillingly suited to the nostalgic melody. It came over powerfully, and was sensuously supported by the humming of the group. The rest of the bar was still and listening. Even the bar-tender had interrupted his serving. He stood with a glass in his hand, the other hand on a pump-handle, and his eyes intent upon the singer. Mimi had created something. With a pub-piano, she had built an experience with an echo.

The song ended; but ignoring applause, she blended the signature notes into *Clopin Clopant*. The transition was faultless, and instead of singing this one she hummed it with a sort of affectionate abandon. Everyone joined her except the bar-tender and me. Nobody now was sitting down the room. They were clustering together with linked arms, swaying and crooning around Mimi. Occasionally she would throw in a few vibrant words, as though the music were recalling to her some blissful memory; and all the time her eyes remained linked to mine, making me an audience of one.

Clopin Clopant finished in a volley of clapping and raucous pleas for more, but this time Mimi rose from the piano, laughing, and picked up a glass that was standing on it.

'That is all, my friends. I have business.'

She pointedly raised the glass to me. I said nothing; she tossed off the drink; it was she who led me through the disappointed customers.

We went out into the hall and she laid her hand on my arm.

'So. Shall we go to your room, or mine?'

I shook my head. 'This isn't social.'

'Not social?'

'No. I have some questions to ask you.'

She gestured carelessly. 'What else? But mustn't we be comfortable while you're asking them?'

'Not so comfortable as you're suggesting.'

'But, my friend, that's a matter of taste. If you don't want to make love to me, foof, foof. But at least, let us discuss it sitting on a bed.'

'We'll discuss it in the office.'

'I don't like the office. To begin with, there is not even a couch. Then there are windows in the door and at the counter. We may as well go back into the bar.'

'At the moment the office happens to be my office.'

'Then I do not admire your taste.'

'I am filled with regret.'

'Huh-huh. How does one fill you with something else?'

I opened the office door and she went in distaste-fully. But then she noticed the curtains for the glass panels.

'Aha. This is not so bad. All it needs now is a soft mattress.'

'Kindly wait here while I fetch my Inspector.'

'But, my friend, for what do we need him?'

'Let us just say to preserve the proprieties.'

She put out her tongue and gave me a V-sign.

I collected Dutt. When we returned, Mimi had drawn the office curtains. She was sitting on a chair turned back-to-front so that her skirt was pushed up to her crotch. She had her arms folded on the back of the chair and was staring maenad-eyed at space. She remained so while we took our seats and while I was leafing through her statement.

'Madame Deslauriers?'

'Uhuh?'

'It would be nice to have your attention.'

She hoisted her shoulders. 'I didn't get yours. Why do you expect me to give you mine?'

'Doesn't the death of your friend matter to you?'

'Can you bring him back to life?'

'I can perhaps discover who killed him. Or don't you really want me to do that?'

She swivelled the chair heavily. 'Monsieur, what good will it do? If this little Rampant killed Freddy, no doubt he is sorry enough now.'

'You don't think he should be punished?'

'He is punished already. He was thinking that Freddy would make him rich. But – pfft! – the job went sour. There was no money for little Rampant.'

'So he was justified in killing Freddy?'

'I do not know about justifications. But he is punished twice, because if there is no Freddy there are no more jobs to do for Freddy. Also, it is in part Freddy's fault. He should not have taken such risks in dealing with Rampant. He should not have made him blow his top, huh? I think that Freddy was a lot to blame.'

'Did Freddy have a temper?'

'Who has not? And it was all the worse because he controlled it. A lawyer, you see. He did it with words. Ah, I can well understand what happened.'

'You are saying he provoked Rampant.'

'But yes. He was very angry after Rampant rang

him. He lay on his bed up there, brooding, planning all he is going to say to him. At the time I am thinking this is perhaps not wise, better let a hard boy handle it for him. But I could not advise Freddy. My wisdom was not to interfere.'

'And this was his mood when he set out.'

She nodded. 'And the rest I understand so well. He skinned this little man, this Rampant; his words were like claws into his brain. He was going to crush him, ha, ha. This Rampant will never cross him again. But they are all alone there. Nobody about. And little Rampant has a knife.'

'You could foresee that.'

'Trouble I saw. I couldn't know it would be so bad.'

'You feared violence.'

'Yes, violence. Freddy's mood is very black.'

'And so he went out on this dangerous mission. He went out, and he didn't come back.'

'Exactly so.'

'Yet you raised no alarm. Why was that, Madame Deslauriers?'

She was still for perhaps two seconds, gazing emptily into nothing. Then she pulled back on the chair in cowboy style and smiled up into my face.

'A trap, huh, pardner?'

'I would like an answer to my question.'

'I think it is a pity you couldn't have questioned Freddy. My God! That would have been a treat. Do you know, in a way you are reminding me of him?'

'You may have time to think, if you wish.'

'He would have said that. He would have been

90

thinking of ways to put me down, make me say what he wanted. Isn't that bizarre?'

I shook my head.

'And you a policeman, he a thief. Uhuh, what is the difference? It is just two teams who play one game.'

'No, Madame Deslauriers.'

'You do not like my paradox?'

'I am afraid this won't do. Either you have your cake or eat it. If you don't decide, I shall.'

'Cake? What cake is that?'

'The cake is your ignorance of the risk that Freddy was taking. That could explain why you raised no alarm. But it excludes you from persuading me that Rampant was the killer.'

She gurgled throatily. 'You think I try to do that?'

'I think you have been trying for the past ten minutes.'

'But it is logical, my friend. And you must admit, convenient. It is not insulting the credibilities.'

'Then why no alarm?'

'Oh foof. Perhaps I am giving it too much drama. I was uneasy, yes, but not too worried. This sort of thing has happened before. Freddy goes away for one, two days. If anyone asks me, I have an excuse. He has gone to view property in Wales, in Cornwall. Freddy was fond of little deals in property.'

'He owned properties?'

'Oh yes, one or two.'

'In Wales, in Cornwall?'

She pulled a glum face. 'Haven't I been telling you that Freddy was secretive? I do not know where his little pieces are.'

'Buying property is legal. Wouldn't he have taken you to visit them?'

'No. His business was not my affair.'

'He just bought them and forgot them?'

'Oh, Freddy forgot nothing. Especially when not to open his mouth.'

'You begin to make me think it's catching,' I said. 'Freddy had property in Scotland. Also a nice villa at Cap Ferrat.'

'The villa, oh yes, the villa. I was thinking you meant in this country.'

'Also in this country. We know of another property.' She drooped her mouth and humped her shoulders.

'Would you like to know where?'

'Should it matter to me?'

'At present it has an occupant.'

'Ah. Freddy let it.'

'I didn't say that. I doubt if this occupant pays any rent.'

She looked askew for a moment. Then she sighed sadly. 'My friend, I can guess what you are trying to tell me.'

'I was sure you could.'

'But I am quite resigned. I have long felt there was another woman.'

'Another woman!'

'But yes. It is not a thing a man can hide. Not even Freddy. I had intimations, you know? The way he was to me in bed.'

'I am not referring to another woman!'

'You try to spare me. You are so kind. But, my

92

friend, it doesn't matter now. All jealousy was over when Freddy died.'

For a space I was silent. I couldn't help it; I had to admire that splendid foil. With style of such an order it was no wonder that Mimi had triumphed over the machinations of her mother-in-law. Nor did she rub it in; she sat mournfully glum, as though bravely accepting her sad thoughts. Not a flicker or gleam in her downcast eye. Nothing to give scepticism a chance.

I threw a look at Dutt: he was studying his notebook.

'Very well,' I said. 'We'll come back to that later.'

'But Monsieur, her name?'

'Never mind her name! What I'd like to talk about now is Bavents.'

Her surprise was perfect. 'The waiter?'

'Indeed yes. The waiter. Who sleeps in a room next to yours. Who blushes when your name is mentioned.'

She gave a little chuckle. 'His name is Adam.'

'I am well aware his name is Adam.'

'He is a dear. A furry animal. I am quite fond of my Adam.'

'So he is your Adam?'

'Am I not saying so? He is feeding out of this hand. It is not a bad idea to enchant the waiter. It ensures the service is dependable.'

'And precisely how far does the enchantment go?'

She did her smiling pull-back on the chair. 'Do not bother to be jealous, my friend. I do not admit Chi-Chi between the sheets. One would need to be butch, huh? All that hair falling over one's face. Oh no. He is for those little thin girls with their drain-pipe bodies and sparrow's legs.'

'But still, the enchantment is pretty strong.'

She gestured. 'Each one has his talent.'

'He would run little errands and keep his mouth shut.'

'How else could he be of service to a lady?'

I drew closer to her. 'And on Thursday evening. Didn't he run a little errand then?'

'An errand for me?'

'An errand to you. From someone requesting a private interview.'

She pretended to think. 'It is not easy to remember. All sorts of funny things go on. One half of the gentlemen staying here keep hinting that they would like a private interview. What would I be doing on Thursday evening?'

'At first you were in the bar with Freddy and the Silvermans.'

'Ah yes, the Silvermans. Tiresome people. Freddy liked them because they were in racing.'

'But then Bavents entered and attracted your attention.'

Her eyebrows lifted. 'You are telling me this?'

'Yes, I'm telling you. And we have a witness. Bavents brought you a message. You went out.'

She swished her hair. 'That is very likely. Yes, I think it may have happened.' She hesitated. 'On Thursday, was it? I wonder what it could have been about?'

'I am sure you know very well what it was about.'

'But no. You had better jog my memory.'

'When you were gone from the bar for over half-an-hour?'

'As long as that?' She made a mouth. 'Where was I, then?'

'You went out in the yard. The man who sent the message was waiting there. You took him aside, perhaps behind those garages, so that you could talk without being seen.'

'Does Adam say this?'

'You had got rid of Adam. Nobody was to hear that conversation. The man had just arrived, he had booked at the Three Tuns. You had to fix him up with a less obvious address.'

'Oh yes, that's certain! I put him under my bed.'

'In point of fact you probably gave him a key.'

'A bedroom key?'

'The key of a front door. With instructions where the door was to be found.'

She shook her head. 'A strange story, my friend. It would surely need proof to make it stand up?'

'Proof – like a statement from the man involved?'

Her eyes flashed quickly, were calm again. 'That would be his word against mine, huh? And how could the word of this man be trusted?'

'You think it couldn't be?'

'Me, I know nothing. These are all your ideas, Monsieur. And I think I hear Freddy say to me, Ignore him, my dear, this is just a try-on.'

'Do you wish to gamble on that?'

Her eyes were hard: then they smiled. 'Yes. I call you.'

'Freddy owned some property just down the river. That was where the door-key fitted.'

Our eyes locked. For a short second I was gazing into the eyes of a furious animal. It passed; she gave her breathless chuckle, dredging it up from deep down.

'I still call you, huh? What do I know of Freddy's properties? And now, if our interesting conversation is to continue, you must be a gentleman and order drinks.'

CHAPTER TEN

I ORDERED DRINKS. Frayling brought them himself; he was doubtless abreast of affairs in the office. He received his reward, if that is what it was, in a melting smile from Madame Deslauriers. He seemed embarrassed. He slopped Dutt's brown ale and got himself tangled with a chair; then he backed out, ducking and grinning. You would almost have taken him for a hot suspect.

Mimi was smiling creamily to herself.

I nodded after Frayling. 'Do you like him better than Bavents?'

'Would it show poor judgement if I did?'

'He has a wife. It could be stupid.'

'Ha, ha, a wife.' She sipped her Martini.

'Perhaps wives don't count in your book.'

'But yes, my friend. I find wives interesting. They are often more bored than the husbands. Sometimes I can put a man in their path.'

'I am sure you favour advanced methods.'

'I prefer not to create a vacuum, huh? After all, I am a woman too. I have every wife's interest at heart.'

I gulped lager. 'And the system works?'

She skewed her mouth. 'Of course, there are failures. Wives who have been paralysed by their one success. These you will find in the divorce courts. But mostly, no. They are simply bored. The big adventure has become routine. And when there are also so many bored husbands, it would be a shame not to spread some happiness. That is logical?'

'It overlooks a few factors.'

'I talk of adventuring, my friend. There is also the grand passion, huh? The love that is proof against all adventures? But that is enfranchising, it does not imprison. The love that imprisons is mere possession. The grand passion has open doors by which we go out and may return.'

'And that was the state of affairs with Freddy?'

She swung her shoulders. 'You know it was not. He was a fascinating man, a tender lover, a good friend. Not more.'

'With your husband, then?'

'Alas no. My marriage to Charles was arranged. He was very charming, but a man of business. I am just his pretty wife waiting on the doorstep.'

'So with whom?'

'Perhaps I am waiting.'

'Or perhaps it is just something you've read in books.'

She drank. 'You are unkind, Monsieur. Why should I tell you all my secrets?'

'Then there is such a man?'

'That is always possible.'

'A man who would undertake grave risks.'

'Maybe.'

'And who is not far away.'

She gazed at me fixedly. 'He may be as close as that chair you are sitting on.'

I grunted and drank more lager. She lifted her glass to me and sipped.

It was growing dark now. I signalled to Dutt, who rose and switched on the light.

'Let us get to something more interesting,' I said. 'When was Freddy proposing to retire?'

Mimi, Madame Deslauriers, had changed her perch on the chair. It could have been that she had judged I had seen enough of her legs. She looked beautifully blank.

'Who says he was retiring?'

'One John Sigismund Fazakerly says it.'

'Oh . . . Siggy.'

'Who you obviously know.'

'But yes.' She faded in a dreamy smile. 'He is the yachtsman who lives in Chelsea. Freddy and he were good friends. Very good-looking, quite rich, but with strange ideas about women.'

'And he says that Freddy was talking about retiring.'

'Aha. But why is that so interesting?'

'Because crooks who retire are a problem to other crooks. Who sometimes make fundamental adjustments.'

She looked studiedly dumb. 'You think that may have happened?'

'First, I would like to hear of his plans for retirement. When; who knew about it; what he had arranged about his mob.'

99

'But, my friend, you ask the wrong person.'

I shook my head. 'I think you would know.'

'It is a matter of business . . .'

'I am not accepting that. My guess is that you were Freddy's reason.'

She smirked faintly. 'You are obstinate, Monsieur. But it comes to the same thing in the end. I do not know what Freddy has planned, or all these other things you are asking.'

'But you knew he was retiring?'

'Very well. It is something we had discussed. After all, Freddy had made his pile. With him, it was getting to the point of being pure art.'

'When did you discuss it?'

'Oh, many times. I had always made my position clear. I did not like Freddy for ever taking such risks. Also, I wished to return to France.'

'So it was largely on your account he bought the villa?'

'But yes. And that was two years ago.'

'He bought it to retire to?'

'That was certainly in his mind. We have never talked of living anywhere else.'

'And you, of course, never urged him to fix a date.'

She flicked her hand. 'Just when he was ready. A little influence, perhaps: I too am a woman. But I am not so naïve as to nag.'

'This summer? The autumn?'

'I think this year. Earlier or later I cannot say.'

'Cannot?'

Her shoulders moved; she tinked the rim of her glass with her nail.

'All right,' I said. 'But this you can tell me. Who did Freddy use to invite to his villa?'

She shifted pose slightly. 'All sorts of people! Once, I believe, he lent it to Siggy.'

'People from London?'

'Not so often. He preferred to mix with the English who live down there. People with money, cars, yachts. Freddy had the style for it. He was liked.'

'Respectable people.'

'Oh yes. Down there he is just another rich man. He is creating an image, you understand. For when all the business is behind him.'

'Yet sometimes he would take acquaintances from London.'

'Well, he knew honest people there, too.'

'Not honest people.'

'He would not take crooks.'

'For example, associates. Like Wicken. Or Fring.'

'Fring?'

'Jimmy Fring.'

She hung on momentarily, her eyes searching. Then she chuckled. 'Ha! Now I understand. It is Jimmy who has the money, huh?'

'You know Fring?'

Her eyes sparkled. 'Of course. I have met them all at some time. Jimmy is a funny one. He is well-educated. He wrote me a poem on a bank-note.'

'And he has been to the villa?'

'I do not know that. No, I should think it is unlikely.'

'Why wouldn't you know?'

'Why should I? I am only at the villa now and then.'

I stared hard at her. 'You'd know, Madame Deslauriers, because the villa was bought on your account. You were the hostess there. It is very improbable that people would visit it without your knowledge.'

She pouted. 'Very well, then. I say no. None of the boys have been to the villa.'

'Not Fring.'

'Not any of them. They perhaps do not know that the villa exists.'

And she looked me straight in the face with frank eyes. The liar.

I took her through her statement. Either it was true or she had the memory of the devil. Nothing was added to that beguiling sketch of innocent crookery gone astray. Quarles had received the message from Rampant; he had majestically programmed and mounted the crime; then disaster had struck. The gang had been shopped, and Quarles slain in a quarrel with Rampant. Simple and logical. What more did I want? Rampant had been taken with blood on his sleeve. Fring and the loot were adrift, certainly, but that was a loose end to tie up at leisure; while sooner or later, suppose it mattered, I might learn the identity of the squeaker.

Simple and logical! Then why confuse it with Peter Robinsons and that malarkey? Which would only turn out, if I chose to pursue it, as an amorous intrigue of poor Mimi's? Mimi had secrets, very well, but it was only the turn of events that had made them seem sinister.

And the more we went over it, the better it sounded. You could feel her poise, her confidence, hardening.

This was the picture: but if it wasn't, who was ever going to prove different?

Nobody, of course.

So we talked it over, her cigarette to my pipe.

'It is truly an irony, my friend. Poor Freddy deserved his success.'

'He was a thief. He left behind him a trail of injured guards and bank officers.'

She issued smoke. 'And that makes him different? Worse than other rich men? The capitalist who steals from the workers and injures them with industrial diseases? No, my friend. Freddy is in step with the moral climate of his culture. His exactions are perhaps less harmful, his initiative more to be admired.'

'An honest thief in a theft-society.'

'That is very nicely put. I am sure you would have liked Freddy. He was a subtle man too.'

I took some puffs. 'I lack his initiative. I am not in the same financial league.'

She sighed. 'No. He was very successful. I think he was perhaps a millionaire.'

'That means there is a lot of money going loose.'

'Oh, I expect he made arrangements. A lawyer, huh? It is not very often that you catch them with their trousers down.'

'A will?'

'That is almost certain.'

'Did Freddy have any close relatives?'

'Uhuh. He had a married sister.' She gave a throbbing laugh. 'I foresee a moral problem there, my friend.'

'How do you mean?'

'She is the wife of a clergyman, I think you call him a rural dean. I have met her, a great hypocrite. She regarded Freddy as dirt.'

'Perhaps she won't inherit.'

'Oh yes, I think so. It would appeal to Freddy's sense of humour. So what is she going to do, poor lady, with all that dirty money in her lily-white hands?'

'Give it away.'

'Aha. Not so easy! She is one with an eye to the main chance. No, I think she will find a way to double-cross her conscience. After all, she is Freddy's sister.'

I floated a smoke-ring. 'Would the money hurt your conscience?'

She chuckled. 'No. But I am a sinner.'

'He may not have made his will for the laughs.'

She hesitated, quizzing me; then shook her head. 'No.. Not possible.'

'Why not possible?'

'You do not understand. Money was never a thing between us. We had a relationship where money was nothing.'

'Yet Freddy loved you.'

'So I expect something, a memento of my poor friend. Shall I tell you what? It will be the Bugatti. And I shall keep it the same, just like Freddy.'

I sped another ring. 'You could never drive it.'

'My friend, I have an eye that creates drivers. The Bugatti will be better than money to me. Perhaps some day soon you are going to return it?'

I shrugged. 'Perhaps. But it isn't yours yet.'

'Oh, I am certain. I shall get the Bugatti.'

'And certain there is a will?'

She leaned her head to one side. 'I do not know that. But wouldn't you?'

End of session.

I sat for a time sucking comfort from a dead pipe, while Dutt lit one of his rare cigarettes (five a day: Iron Len). It was nearly midnight. Three hours of Mimi, and she had left as sprightly as she had come. And why not? On the judges' cards she had probably earned a majority verdict. I tried a fresh match, got a raw, wet taste, and certified the pipe as a goner.

'Did you notice anything useful?'

Dutt carburetted smoke. 'She struck me as being a cool one, sir.'

'I don't need Einstein to tell me that. What did you spot that I might have missed?'

'Well, sir.' Dutt eased his seat. 'I thought you had her going a couple of times. Once about her failing to raise the alarm, and once when you were sprucing her about a statement from chummie.'

'But especially the latter.'

'As you say, sir. And the two do go together. Though I reckon we shan't be getting much ahead until we can lay our hands on him.'

I nodded. 'That's the break we need.'

'It will clear it up, one way or the other.'

I stared. 'Are you going along with the lady?'

Dutt humped his shoulders and looked stupid.

Then the phone went. I hooked it up; Dainty was at the other end.

'Hallo? Haven't you managed to get to bed yet?'

'Cut the comedy,' I said. 'It's too late.'

I could hear his mates cackling in the background.

'No, listen,' he said. 'We've something for you. This Peter Robinson. There's a chummie called Bilney. He's been adrift a few days. He could fit.'

'Does he match the description?'

'Who doesn't? But I'd say he matches it as well as most. Thirty, fair hair, sideboards. I'm sending you the bumf on teletype.'

'What makes him a candidate?'

'He's missing, for one. For two, he's an associate of Wicken's. May have done a job or two with Quarles. He hangs around the fringe of the gangs.'

It sounded promising. 'What's his form?'

'He's done some porridge for G.B.H. I'm told he has a nasty temper, has been known to use a knife.'

'Is he left-handed?'

'Get knotted,' Dainty said. 'The fine print is coming over the wire. I just thought I might catch you between rounds.'

'Ha, ha,' I said. 'Go to hell.'

CHAPTER ELEVEN

B UT GIVE DAINTY a mark for prescience: there was indeed a late-night comedy interlude.

When we broke up, Dutt went for a bath; I decided mine could wait till morning.

I got into bed and lay brooding a while over the twists and nuances of the case. I find that when I'm relaxed, horizontal, and about to drop off, the facts will sometimes sort themselves without help from me. It is as though, at that point, they take on a life of their own, and begin to exhibit aspects that till then I've been blind to; but it may be simply that I am resting the intellect and permitting the intuition to have free play. Moments of sartori, involuntary Zen: a genius is a man who has learned to switch off.

So I was lying like that, trying to be a genius, when I heard Dutt's slippers slopping back along the corridor; then the sound of him opening his door, which apparently he had left unlocked (a policeman's mind is never still). Followed confused sounds, and a tap at my door. I switched on the bed-light. Dutt entered. His face was pink, and he was grappling his dressing-gown round him with a curiously intent modesty.

'Sir . . . could you spare a moment?'

I climbed into a dressing-gown and we went to his room. Sitting-up in the bed, and sensationally naked, was Mimi, Madame Deslauriers. She regarded us with mild surprise.

'This is flattering. But shouldn't one of you gentlemen retire?'

'Get out of it,' I said. 'You've picked the wrong room. Mine is across the corridor.'

'This is not your room?'

'It's the Inspector's.'

She said something rapidly, in French. 'It is that stupid yak, he tells me wrong. I will give him a hair-cut with a blow-torch.'

'So kindly hook it.'

She got out of the bed and stood for a moment, nudely glaring. But then she burst into gurgling laughter.

'This is formidable, don't you agree?'

'I don't agree.'

'The poor Dutt. And he is a family man, huh?'

'Never mind about Dutt. Just slip into this.' I picked a frothy black night-dress from a chair by the bed.

She took the night-dress but didn't slip into it.

'Monsieur, it is the mistake which has made you angry. But that is easily put right. I will cross the corridor. Let us leave the poor Dutt to his honest slumbers.'

'I just want you to scram.'

'Oh, but no. When I am so convenient and agreeable. All day you are making the impression, huh? You must not be impolite now.'

'But I haven't been making the impression!'

'Oh yes, yes. In your policeman's way.'

'Look,' I said. 'Put it on or leave it off, but get back to your room – or I'll call the manager.'

She looked at me sadly. 'That is not being serious.'

'Yes it is. I want you gone.'

'No. The mistake, that is the trouble. You have wished my visit to be more discreet. But now I tell you. I will go away. I will do exactly as the man says.' She gave me a lightning wink. 'Poor Mimi. This has not been her lucky day.'

She slid the night-dress over her head – which was an erotic act on its own – smiled apologetically at Dutt, and cruised regally out of the room.

Dutt goggled after her.

'Do you think she'll be back, sir?'

'That appeared to be the message. We had better bolt our doors.'

'You bet, sir!'

But Mimi didn't come back.

Hanson's messenger delivered the Bilney dossier at breakfast the next morning. It made no mention of Bilney's being left-handed, but the other details fitted rather well.

Bilney, Thomas Henry. Age 30. 5′ 10½″, strong build. Fair hair, grey eyes, narrow features, small ears. 2″ scar left cheek. Missing top joint of little finger, left. London accent. Born, Lambeth. P.O.A., Shepherd's Bush. Last seen, Thursday. Total of six years for G.B.H. and robbery with violence.

The photographs showed a good-looking villain,

one who might well appeal to the ladies; but there was violence in the mouth, which was small, and in the prominence of the blunt chin (check fifty or so photographs of convicted murderers and you will find that Lombroso wasn't far out). The eyes were glazed-looking, avoiding the camera. He had thick eyebrows but scanty lashes. The scar, nearly vertical, was certainly a knife-slash, and he may have lost the finger-joint in parrying the attack.

I showed the photographs to Dutt.

'Would you let him buy you a drink?'

Dutt grinned. 'Only for a cover while I was getting out the cuffs, sir.'

'Do you know him?'

'No sir. But I know a lot like him. And when his type are around I'm careful not to turn my back.'

Mimi was seated at her table, looking gorgeous in white leather hot pants. I took the photographs along to her and sat myself in the chair opposite. She was eating grapefruit. She gave the grapefruit a dig, sending a spurt in my direction. I gravely blotted the juice with a napkin before exhibiting the photographs.

'A friend sent me these.'

She gave them a glance. 'Monsieur enjoys a distinguished acquaintance.'

'His name is Tom,' I said. 'I am wondering if you can guess his age.'

She took a longer look; but if there was a tremor of recognition I failed to detect it. Or anything else. She was keeping her face completely vacant, an unregistering mask.

'I would guess he was seven.'

'That's his mental age.'

'So then. You will have much in common.'

'Have you any message for him?'

'Please go away,' she said. 'I wish to continue with my breakfast.'

So I switched to Bavents, who I waylaid as he came through the swing doors from the kitchen. He was juggling with a tray and a covered dish: I shepherded him into the chef's corner.

'Take a look at these.'

I made a fan of the photographs and held them close to his pink nose. The tray and the dish chattered.

'I – I don't know anyone like that!'

I clicked my tongue. 'You were talking to him on Thursday.'

'No! I've n-never seen him before.'

'Not Tom Bilney? Who slipped you the quid?'

'No, it's the truth! I've never m-met him.'

'But he did slip you a quid?'

'He d-didn't, I tell you!'

'So how much was it? Fifty pence?'

'I – no, n-nothing! I d-didn't see anyone!'

I left off before he dropped the tray.

But I was luckier after breakfast, when I paid a visit to the Three Tuns. Both Eddie Jimpson, the licensee, and his wife Doris had had avowed contact with 'Peter Robinson'. On Thursday Eddie had been serving in the bar, and he had passed on the man to Doris. Doris had booked him in and taken him up to show him his room.

'Could this have been the man?'

111

They went into a huddle over the photographs.

'It's like him,' Eddie said. 'He's fair, isn't he?'

'Fair. Grey eyes. About five feet ten.'

'This one was big with it,' Eddie said. 'Looked as though he could be a rum customer.'

'This one is big with it. He can be rum.'

'Then I reckon it's the same man.'

I looked at Doris. 'What do you say?'

Doris, plump and curly, was frowning.

'I don't know what to say. It could be him, but it isn't easy to tell from a photograph.'

I whipped the photographs away. 'Describe your man.' Doris leaned her haunch against the bar. 'Well, he was fair all right, and I didn't much like him. He'd got dead sort of eyes. You were just muck to him.'

'Any special features?'

'Not that I remember. Though of course you could tell he was a cockney.'

'Eddie?'

Eddie shook his head. 'That's what I was going to say,' he said.

'Try thinking about his face. Just let it come to mind, don't force yourself into seeing it.'

'He was looking a bit scruffy,' Doris said, after a moment. 'Sweaty. Like he might have been driving all day.'

'Sweaty and grimy?'

'A bit of that too. You'd have thought he would have washed before he went out.'

'But in the morning, at breakfast, he would be tidied up?'

'Well yes, he was smart enough then.'

Could they have missed the scar? It wasn't very prominent, except perhaps to an eye conditioned like mine: it followed the natural lines of the face, it might register without at first being recognized. As for the missing joint, he would keep that inconspicuous.

'Did you watch him sign the book?'

'Of course.'

'Did he use his right hand or his left?'

Doris gestured helplessly. 'If he had used his left hand, I should think I would've noticed that.'

'Anything else about his hands?'

'They weren't very clean.'

'Do you mind if I see the book?'

Doris fetched it. The 'Peter Robinson' entry had been made in bold but back-slanted writing. No visible dabs, and a poor paper for latents: not much to hope for from that.

'What I would like to see now is the room where he slept.'

'The room has been let again, you know.'

I sighed to myself. 'Never mind. Just ask the occupant if I may step in.'

In fact, the occupant was out. Doris used her pass-key to admit me to a small, pleasant room, the single window of which was framing a view of a giant chestnut in lavish bloom. It was fitted with a wash-basin, mirror, a glass shelf and a tooth-glass located in a chromium-plated holder. The paint was clean and shiny on the frame of the sash-window, a white-enamelled dressing-table, and the door.

'Who serviced the room after he left?'

'I did,' Doris said.

'Tell me what you did.'

'I changed the bed-linen, hoovered, dusted and gave it all a wipe over.'

'How much is all?'

'Well, the wash-basin mostly; the shelf, the mirror. And I changed the glass.'

'Did you touch the paintwork?'

'Only with a duster. The paint was washed a fort-night ago.'

Which sounded like a frost; but to turn every stone, I rang Hanson to send out a dabs team. They arrived within half-an-hour. I gave them the register and turned them loose in the little bedroom. A lot of insufflating and snazzy camera-work and paint left looking as though the devil had stroked it; then Eddie, Doris and the apprehensive room-occupant were check-printed for comparisons. Results: nil. Bilney wasn't yet a certainty, just a hot front-runner. One witness liked him, one was cautious. But I felt the wind was blowing his way.

And the more so when I returned to the Barge-House, where Dutt was just putting down the phone.

'That was Dainty, sir.'

'Has he collared Fring yet?'

'No sir. But he's been chatting-up Bilney's girl-friend.'

I shrugged and sat. The girl-friends of villains are a highly variable quantity. Even when they are jealous their information is suspect, and in the normal way they simply go dumb.

'Why has this one suddenly turned chatty?'

'Dainty says it's because she's scared.'

'Scared of what?'

'Of Bilney's being missing, sir. She reckons he ought to be back by now.'

I grunted. But somebody might love Bilney.

'What's this girl-friend's name and trade?'

'Name is Mavis Treadwell, sir, and she claims to be a photographer's model. It seems she had a date with Bilney for Friday. She has a key to his flat in the Bush. When she arrived there she found he'd left a note for her saying he'd been called away on a job.'

'On a job?'

'Well, that's what she infers, sir. And she's the one who should know. But the point is he's been gone for three or four days now, and she reckons that something must have happened to him.'

'Then she knows more than she's saying.'

'Dainty thinks not, sir. She's sure Bilney would have rung her before now. All the other jobs he's done have been in the locality. He's never been away so long before.'

'Any inkling of what job?'

'Afraid not, sir.'

'Had she any idea of where he was heading?'

Dutt shook his head. 'I did put some questions, sir. But what I told you was all Dainty had got.'

I drew invisible lines on Frayling's desk. The picture was growing.

'It would be on Thursday that Bilney left the note.'

'Yes, sir. Dainty did go into that. Treadwell says the note wasn't dated. She'd last seen Bilney on Wednesday evening.'

'So on Thursday someone called him up here, and we assume he was the man who booked in at the Three Tuns. His first move then was to contact Deslauriers. There can't be much doubt about what the job was.'

'Not very much, sir.' Dutt looked glum.

'Then Deslauriers installed him in Freddy's hideaway. On Friday the trouble with Rampant provided an opportunity, and Deslauriers phoned Bilney with instructions. Straightforward so far?'

Dutt nodded.

'Bilney did the job and returned to the hideaway. But now we have a problem. Bilney stayed put. He didn't hurry back to home and Mavis. Why would that be?'

Dutt puckered his eyes. 'Could he have been on the same lark as Rampant?'

'You mean blackmail?'

'He might have had a bash at it. His sort don't go in much for brains.'

I considered it. 'It's the simple answer, and it fits with Deslauriers secretly meeting him. But she must have warned him yesterday that I nearly caught her with him. You would think he would be back home by now.'

Dutt hunched a shoulder. 'Some of them are thick. Perhaps he thinks the pressure will make her cough up.'

'The alternative is that Bilney is her boy-friend. Which raises another problem. I can't believe it.'

A tap at the door interrupted the conference; semi-handsome Hanson stalked in. He was looking happy.

He leered at each of us before sprawling himself on the third chair.

'Are you still wanting Bilney?'

I stared. 'Have you got him?'

'Well, maybe not yet under lock and key. But we've found his little paw marks at Raynham. I thought you might like to come along.'

CHAPTER TWELVE

'P AW MARKS' WAS a metaphor: at that precise
juncture all Hanson had was a missing person.
But the person was missing from a riverside inn, and
the description mentioned a scar and an amputated
finger-joint. Furthermore, Raynham was the next
village downstream from Sallowes; the inn, the
Reed-Cutters, stood opposite the staithe. Bilney, now
using the pseudonym of H. Wilson, had booked in
there on the Friday evening.

'One of the County men called there yesterday,'
Hanson explained. 'We thought the description
sounded interesting. But chummie was out. When
we called this morning the publican told us he hadn't
come back.'

'Did he leave his gear?'

'So I'm told. He must have got word from the lady
and skarpered. But this description of Bilney is a snap
fit. There can't be two like him swanning around. Is
Friday right?'

'Friday is right.'

'Then it looks like this case is falling together.' He

plucked his lip. 'A pity, really. I was tipping you to get round to Rampant in the end.' He got to his feet. 'Shall we go?'

'First, I want a man and a car.'

'Huh?' Hanson looked aggrieved.

'We'll need to leave this place covered. If Bilney's on the loose, this is where he may head for.'

In the end I got a van and two men, with a third man to cover the river approach. Dutt I left with the special mission of keeping his willing eye on Mimi.

Raynham was nine country miles from Haughton. It was a small village on a bluff by a broad; its handsome church tower stood high among trees, with below it pantiled cottages and infillings of bungalows. The broad was small and fly-blown with hire craft, a handful of yachts in a slum of motor-cruisers. An ugly beard of battered craft fringed the tiny staithe, which was itself parked solid with the cars of day-visitors. Facing the stage was a cramped junction and in one of its angles stood the Reed-Cutters. Two police cars were parked on the handkerchief of frontage, leaving bare room for us to slot in too. Hanson rammed us home. We got out.

'Welcome to Mug's Corner,' Hanson said sourly. 'Once I kept a half-decker in the dyke here. The second time they sank it I gave up.'

'But it looks a good spot for a chummie to hole-up in.'

'Oh sure.' He stared about savagely. 'These are the conditions of crime, sonny. Greed-pollution. Maybe it's time we had another war.'

We pushed into the bar, where there was standing-room only, and through a door to the back premises. Hanson introduced me to the licensee, Silkin, and the County C.I.D. man, Inspector Breckles. Silkin was a heavy, fresh-faced countryman, Breckles a cherub with watchful eyes. We pulled up seats round a massive table; I spread out the Bilney photographs in front of Silkin.

'Is this your customer, H. Wilson?'

Silkin looked them over. 'Yes, that's him, sir.'

'What made you notice his little finger?'

Silkin blew out his cheeks. 'Don't rightly know, sir.'

'Did you see it when he filled in the register?'

'No. Because I filled it in myself.'

'Did you see him write anything?'

Silkin looked puzzled. 'Now you mention it, I don't think I did. I reckon I noticed that finger when he was sinking a pint, that's the time when I saw most of him.'

A left-handed drinker.

'Was he in the bar a lot?'

'I'm telling a lie, sir. He wasn't in often. Just last thing he'd come in for a couple, and then go straight up to bed.'

'Did he talk to anyone?'

'That's difficult to say, with all the crowd we get in here. But I can't say I noticed he was very sociable. He never said much to me or the missus.'

'What about phone calls?'

'He didn't make any here.'

'Did he receive any?'

Silkin shook his head. 'But there's a phone-box a

120

few yards up the road. He could have used that if he wanted to be private.'

For out-going calls . . . but the others?

'What did he do with himself all day?'

Silkin puffed his cheeks. 'I reckon you'll have to tell me, sir. He was out of here each day after he'd had his breakfast.'

'He went out in his car?'

'He did if he had one.'

'But surely you know if he had a car?'

'The guests park over the way, sir,' Inspector Breckles put in. 'There's no room this side. I've sent a man to make enquiries.'

'They leave their cars on the staithe?'

'That's right,' Silkin said. 'And that's where this man would've left his. But there's always a dozen or more left across there, so whether he had one I couldn't say.'

'A blue Viva,' Hanson said. 'Of course the bloody car was across there.'

Silkin stuck out his chin mulishly. Hanson never had charm to spare for the natives.

'Let's go back to Friday,' I said hastily. 'When did this fellow arrive here?'

'It was three to three-thirty,' Silkin said grumpily. 'We were having a bite after the bar closed. He came through the yard and knocked on the door. Asked if we could put him up for a few days.'

'A few days?'

'Those were his words. Told me he was here on a bit of business. He offered to pay me in advance, but like a fool I didn't accept it.'

'Did he have his case with him?' Hanson snapped.

Silkin sniffed. 'He fetched it afterwards.'

'So like that wouldn't he have had a car outside?'

Silkin humped his shoulders. 'It must have been my dull day.'

Hanson snorted: I shot him a quick look.

'What happened after you had booked him in?'

Silkin sniffed again. 'He went out, didn't he? Said he'd see us later, then he went out.'

'When did he come back?'

'Well, it was latish. He came into the bar near closing-time. He had his couple, the way I told you, and went up while I was still doing the till.'

I paused. 'You are sure you didn't see him earlier?'

His eye met mine. 'Quite sure of it, sir.'

'Your wife?'

'She wouldn't have seen him till closing. She was in the back when he came in.'

'You understand what these questions are about. That you may have to repeat what you're telling me on oath?'

'Yes, sir. Inspector Breckles informed me. But that fellow wasn't back here till turned ten.'

So there it was: barring an alibi, which Bilney wouldn't find easy in a strange manor.

'Did you notice anything special about him that night?'

Silkin hesitated. 'He may have looked a bit untidy.'

'How, untidy?'

'Well, his hair was ruffled, and maybe his clothes a bit creased.'

'No blood on his sleeve?' Hanson cut in.

Silkin looked shocked. 'I didn't see blood. I'm trying to tell you what I can remember. I can't do better for you than that.'

'What about his manner?' I asked.

Silkin blew into his cheeks. 'I just served him. I didn't notice.'

'Was his hand trembling?'

'I didn't notice. When I think of any more, I'll tell you.' I silently cursed Hanson.

'Now I'd like you to tell me about yesterday. What time did Bilney go out?'

Silkin's eyes were sullen. 'His usual time. After breakfast.'

'Wasn't it a little later yesterday?'

'No, it wasn't. It was how I said.'

'Didn't he receive a phone call?'

'I told you he didn't. Now I want to go through there and help the missus.'

'You'd better go then.'

Silkin hesitated briefly before hauling himself up and clumping out. Hanson stared after him evilly. Breckles gave me a quizzical glance.

We went up to the bedroom by a crooked stair that had a rope for a hand-rail. A different dabs-team was at work there, and this time no check-printing was necessary. On the door, the tooth-glass and Bilney's Remington razor were prints matching those that had come over the wire. Bilney was in. Hanson had already sent out a general W.F.Q. alert.

We turned over Bilney's gear, which suggested that he hadn't anticipated a lengthy stay out of town. In a squash-top suitcase were a soiled change of underwear, a screw of bennies and two pornographic paperbacks. No spare shoes, ties or socks. A raincoat he might have kept in the car. His toilet stuff was the bare minimum and didn't run to talcum or after-shave.

Hanson sprawled gracelessly on the bed. 'What does Scotland Yard make of it?'

I shrugged and fed Erinmore into my pipe. I wasn't quite sure what I was making of it: my intuition was failing to click. But I had a feeling of sadness about that little room, about the paltry possessions Bilney had abandoned there. Almost feeling sorry for the stupid jerk: an emotion he wouldn't have wasted on me.

Hanson lit a cheroot. 'Do you want my opinion?'

I borrowed his matches. 'Why not?'

'I'd say chummie came out here to do a quick job, but then he got hooked with a different angle.'

Hanson and Dutt, both.

'Of course, you mean blackmail.'

Hanson horsed smoke. 'What's wrong with that? Deslauriers has money. She ordered a killing. Which left her wide open for a big touch.'

I tossed back the matches. 'No touch is worth a lifer. Bilney could only shop her by shopping himself.'

'Yeah, that's how you think, that's how I think. But we're talking of a buster with his brains in his knuckles.' He spat some cheroot. 'Look, chummie does his job, but he doesn't go home the way he planned to. Then what's holding him here? What's the attraction? With the police busting a gut all around?'

I puffed twice. 'Say he's sweet on the lady.'

'Ha bloody ha,' Hanson jeered. 'You know there's only one attraction for a louse like Bilney, and that's the stuff that comes out of banks. He's putting the black on, and this is the place for it, where the lady has to act all sweet and innocent. She's wanting him gone and long gone. Every day he stops here is a boost to the pressure.'

'It fits some of the facts.'

'You bet it fits them. Bilney wasn't risking any lifer. She had to pay him to go away, to stop giving us notions. That was the deal he was sitting in with.'

'And now he's gone.'

'Yeah, now he's gone.' Hanson sucked and spat out more leaf. 'So either the lady paid him off, or more likely your coming on the scene scared him.'

'You're saying she warned him.'

'Yeah.'

'How?'

Hanson stared. 'How should I know how? You let her go back to the hotel before you. She would have had time to put in a call.'

I shook my head decidedly. 'It can't be that simple. Bilney didn't return to base after meeting her. And he wouldn't spend his days camping-out in a call-box, waiting for the lady to ring him warnings.'

'Then she used a messenger. Maybe that long-hair.'

'Bavents?'

'Yeah. Didn't I hear he was wet on her?'

I sieved a puff; Bavents was a possible. I wasn't at all sure of my ranking of Bavents.

'It would mean letting someone else into the know, and the lady is too intelligent to want that to happen.

In fact, the lady is too intelligent, period. She would never let Bilney get away with blacking her.'

'Balls. She would be in a cleft stick.'

'So she would get on the phone. But not to Bilney.'

Hanson smoked ferociously, but it was a point. Cheaper to buy muscle than pay black.

'All right, then. Suppose I'm wrong. You tell me why chummie hangs on here.'

I launched smoke at the small lattice window that overlooked the road, the jammed staithe, the jammed broad.

'I don't know. I've been wrong too. Deslauriers didn't send Bilney to Freddy's hideaway. And according to Silkin Bilney received no phone calls, yet Deslauriers must have phoned him at least once. That could have been a call by appointment, but if so the timing was strangely felicitous. And if it happened again yesterday, after she met me, then felicitous stops describing it.'

Hanson wriggled. 'So what's the next move?'

'Bilney hadn't returned to town this morning.'

'Meaning he's still here?'

'We had better assume that. And assume also that he's still in touch with the lady.' I puffed. 'What would you do in her place?'

'Me?' Hanson champed on the cheroot. 'I'd get him out of circulation fast. It's too late in the game to leave him around loose.'

'And where would you put him?'

He sighed smoke. 'This time it has to be Hernando's Hideaway. But for crying out loud, we've been doing our nuts over it. Maybe you'd better call in the Army.'

We went back down into the parlour. Hanson had a map fetched from the car. We spread it out on Silkin's great mahogany dining-table and clustered round it in a hopeful seance. Breckles, the local man, pointed out the venues of holiday-bungalow development. They peppered the river-banks for miles and choked minor backwaters and tributaries. Then there were boatyards and mooring dykes where house-boats were lodged in their dozens. The Army wasn't such a bad idea; a thorough check of the riverside might take weeks.

'Have you been in touch with the rating department?'

'Yes, sir,' Breckles said. 'They are getting out lists for us, all the properties with registered owners in the London district.'

'Roughly how many?'

'Over two thousand, sir. And we're getting lists of house-boat owners from the River Commissioners. But it's all taking a bit of time. I reckon the men on the spot have got the best chance.'

Perhaps.

'You're a native here, aren't you?'

'That's right, sir. Born in Haughton.'

'Right. Now forget the map. Just close your eyes and think of the river. The quiet, hidden places. Places that for some reason missed being developed. Maybe ruinous, ramshackle places. Silted-up dykes, too shallow to navigate. Lonely; poor access; barely good enough to get a car down. Are you doing that?'

'I'm trying, sir.'

'Then make me a list of all those places.'

'Yes, sir. I'll certainly try.'

Hanson's expression said I'd never rated lower.

CHAPTER THIRTEEN

Silkin's wife supplied us with sandwiches and we took them, with bottles, to a bench across the road; not on the staithe, but beside a mooring cut used by the trip-boats to decant their pay-load. A path led to the cut through a grove of alders, and the bench stood in the shade of the grove. Except for a mound of dredged mud that lay steaming on the bank the spot was pleasant, being screened from the broad.

We ate and drank silently. Hanson had a dreamy expression. He was beginning to see the end of this case. Our discoveries at Raynham had reduced it to a routine-matter – time-wasting, of course, but no longer speculative. Sooner or later, most probably sooner, we would have Bilney tucked away in the cooler; and with any sort of policeman's luck, enough hard evidence for a copper-bottomed case. Like the knife, like blood on sleeves. Bilney would be fortunate if we didn't find something. And with Bilney in the cooler we could play him against Deslauriers, and Deslauriers against him – routine, routine!

Then why wasn't I feeling happy too, who didn't

have to bother even with the routine? A few loose ends? But every case has them. Otherwise defence counsels would go out of business. So I didn't know how Deslauriers communicated with Bilney – well, no doubt I would know, later. And I didn't know why Bilney stayed around after the job – well, there were a couple of theories covering that. Then there was the right-hand, left-hand business: wasn't I attaching too much importance to it? If it wouldn't throw a jury (and it wouldn't), had I any right to let it throw me? No: when you added it all together, I had no grounds for feeling so pensive over my sandwiches. From the moment we had tied Bilney into the case its main outlines were cut and dried.

I finished my bottle, and Hanson offered me one of his sin-black Burmese cheroots. While I was light-ing it we were joined by the man who had been sent to make enquiries at the staithe. He had had no luck. About twenty cars were left parked on the staithe every night, some from the guest-house up the road, some belonging to vacationists who rented the cottages. Nobody specifically remembered a blue Viva, though some remembered cars that were blue. Among them Bilney's, without doubt. Only a Viva-driver notices another Viva.

'Did anyone remember seeing Bilney himself?'

'Yes, sir. He used the shop on the staithe a few times. He bought his fags and newspapers there. The lady who runs it gave a good description.'

'At what times was he in there?'

'In the morning, sir. And it was the local paper he bought.'

Naturally. 'Did she notice his hand?'

'Yes, sir. Also his scar.'

I ran it through my mind: Bilney buying a paper, feeling in his pocket for a coin. If he had felt with his right hand, holding the paper in his left, would the lady have been able to see that finger? But he had bought cigarettes there, too, putting out his left hand as he tended with his right – or vice versa: and either way, giving her a sight of the finger.

'Is there a garage in Raynham?'

'No, sir. The nearest is in Sallowes.'

'Call in and enquire if he bought petrol there. With special reference to Friday evening.'

The man ducked and went; Hanson dragged smoke; a trip-boat came nosing up the cut. We watched her naval-suited crew moor her to two posts, then got out ahead of the crowd.

In Silkin's parlour Breckles was still sitting with the map spread out before him, but now a number of red ball-pen carrots had been neatly marked upon it. Breckles rose as we entered.

'I've had a shot at your idea, sir.'

'Are these your probables?'

'I wouldn't like to say that, sir. But there's a couple we could take a look at. I've just been checking with the Rates Department and two of these places have London-registered owners. One is a private person with a Kensington address, the other is a holding company in Balham.'

'And where are those places?'

'Both near here, sir. This one is Blackdyke Fen, at

Beastwick. Then there's Turnpudden Hole, between Sallowes and Wrackstead. Both of them are pretty well off the map.'

'Which is your choice?'

Breckles shrugged embarrassedly. 'I'd say it was all a bit of guess-work, sir. Turnpudden Hole is nearest to Wrackstead, but I can't think how a Londoner would get to know about it.'

'It's part of the old Gifford estate,' Hanson said. 'The estate was sold up after the war. A development company bought a lot of it, all the fens down that side.'

'What about the other place?'

'Perhaps more likely,' Breckles said. 'But I wouldn't care to bet on that, either. It's a converted mill right out on the marshes. As far as I know it isn't being lived in.'

'But that one is privately owned?'

'Yes, sir.' Breckles took out a notebook and flipped the pages. 'E. V. Selkirk, 73 Glebe Road, Kensington. He's been the owner since '68.'

I looked at Hanson. 'Any preference?'

Hanson chewed his cheroot unhelpfully.

'Right then,' I said. 'We'll try the mill.'

Hanson opened and closed his bony hand.

We collected a fourth man and drove to Beastwick, a pretty village with its back to the river. The cottages were styled in Art Nouveau rustic, but grouped with a keen eye for effect. We entered a skein of jumbled lanes, with the marsh and carr hazy below us, and came at last to a humpy marsh track, where marl combined with flints and brickbats.

'How much further?' I asked Breckles.

'It'll be about another quarter of a mile, sir.'

'Any cover?'

'There's alder carrs, sir. But you'll maybe go in up to your backside.'

'Is there any other way out besides this?'

'No sir, unless chummie has got a boat. But I passed by on a River Patrol launch last week, and the cut was empty then.'

'Suppose he is a swimmer?'

Breckles shook his head. 'It's all carrs and marshes, both sides. He might lose himself in there for a couple of days, but he would be damned glad to come out after that. If he takes to the marshes, we'll have him.'

'Unless he steps into a mud-hole,' Hanson said.

We bumbled on a short way further, then I halted and parked to block the track. Just there it was running through thick groves of alder in-filled with willow brush and sedge. Off the track it was sloughy black peat-mud; the air was sweatily humid and smelling of mint. The four of us alighting disturbed a jay, which blundered off through the twigs with klaxon-like cries.

'Christ,' Hanson muttered. 'That should tell him!'

We waited by the car for a couple of minutes. Once the jay had settled the carrs fell silent: just the murmur of mosquitoes that had come to inspect us.

'You lead,' I said to Breckles.

We followed him down the track at twenty yards distance. The track made a slow turn through the alders and brought into view the tops of giant willows. Breckles signalled us to wait. He edged cautiously forward, was lost to sight behind a screen of scrub willow. We stood moistly flipping at the mosquitoes for what seemed an unnecessary interval. Then Breckles reappeared, waving to us. We joined him beside the scrub willow. Peering round it, we could see the brick mill-tower standing among the tall willows, with the river beyond.

'I don't think he's at home,' Breckles whispered. 'I've been up to have a squint in the garage.'

He indicated a sagging out-building with a roof of reed thatch, which was beginning to shed.

'Any signs of use?'

'None I've seen. But you would expect chummie to play it clever. He may have parked his car on the hard-standing. You would never spot it from the river.'

I grunted and took in the scene. Once, someone had spent a lot of money on the mill. Fresh windows had been pierced at each of its four stories and a circular, white-painted verandah constructed around the cap. Once, too, there had been a lawn under the willows, trellised roses, a quay-heading. The mill-dyke had been enlarged and piled and had doubtless housed a launch or a motor-cruiser. Once. But not now. Now, the jungle was taking it back. The white paint was flaking, the quay-headings ruinous, and persicaria blooming in the silted-up dyke. And it gave an impression of intense loneliness, of a far-off outpost that had died. If it wasn't haunted, it ought to be. A place fit only for ghosts.

'Where is the door?'

'It faces the river.'

'Let's spread out and take a look.'

Dyke, marsh and undergrowth prevented us from surrounding the mill, but we did our best with what was left. I crossed a shaky bridge and followed a tiled path, of which the pemmons were sinking and choked with grass. It brought me to a shabby door. The door was secured with a massive rusty chain and a rusty padlock. Breckles joined me.

'Is this the only entry?'

'There's a ground-floor window, sir. But it looks intact.'

'Would you say this door had been unlocked since Christmas?'

Breckles poked the padlock, and swallowed. 'No, sir.'

But we were there, so we went through the motions. Hanson thumped the door and called on Bilney to come out. He disturbed the jay again. It went clamouring through the carrs like a panicky blackbird with roup. Then silence.

'We have tools, sir,' Breckles ventured. 'I could get that lock off in two minutes.'

I looked at Breckles, Breckles looked at his feet.

We went back to the car.

Before we set out on our second goose-hunt I rang Dutt from a box in the village. Dutt had seen no more of Bilney than we had and could offer only minor and marginal information. Dainty had rung. The French police at Cap Ferrat had paid a call at Freddy's villa. It was empty, but they had found signs of a very recent occupation. The caretaker, a retired procuress from

Marseilles, had attempted to explain this by admitting to the illicit entertainment of friends there; the French police had pretended to accept the explanation. They were now keeping a close watch on the villa.

'Any word of Bilney from Shepherd's Bush?'

'No, sir. But they've posted a man at his flat.'

'What has the lady been doing?'

'She's been shopping, sir. She bought two blouses and a George Formby record. Then she went up to her room and played the record, and about half-past twelve she must have rung for a drink. Bavents fetched it, a Dubonnet and lemon, and he was in her room about twenty minutes.'

'Was your ear to the key-hole?'

'Well, actually, yes, sir. But all I could hear was that blooming record. First it was *If Women Like Them* and then *Swimmin With The Women.*'

I clicked my tongue. 'She's adding to her repertoire. Has Bavents gone out or made any phone calls?'

'No, sir. He was serving at lunch, and now he's in the kitchen manicuring vegetables.'

Which sounded innocent enough, unless one remembered that he would be fixing the veg with his left hand.

I rejoined the others in the car and we went on our way to Turnpudden Hole. Nobody was saying much. Breckles in particular had a droopy expression on his round-cheeked face. Hanson was silently savaging a cheroot. The D.C., who was driving, stared over his bonnet. I chewed my pipe-stem. We passed through Sallowes and turned once more into the lanes.

'What sort of place is Turnpudden Hole?'

Breckles made a little gesture with one shoulder. 'It's just a small broad, sir. Mostly grown over. The old blokes used to say it was bottomless.'

'But is there a house or something?'

Hanson gnashed smoke. 'There's a shack they put up for Clytie Gifford. She was a weirdo, an eccentric. Liked to live alone with the birds.'

'And it's been empty for some time?'

'Yeah. Clytie pegged out soon after the war. Then the estate was sold up. Only a nut could live out there.'

I left it at that. But what I had been noticing were telephone posts marching beside us. They stayed with us through a plantation of larches before turning right, across a field. In a little distance we also turned right, to find our way barred by a ramshackle field-gate; the D.C. made to get out to open it: I stopped him and climbed out myself. I prowled round the gate. At first, I saw nothing. The gate was secured by a chain and staple; a shag of ivy had grown up the hinge-post and was sending a tendril along the top bar. Then I spotted a scrape, slight but definite, where the gate had brushed the crown of the track; and when I came to unhook the chain there was a glint of silver where it left the staple.

I got back in the car.

'The gate has been used lately.'

Hanson sniffed. 'So what does that tell us?'

'It tells us the gate has been used lately.'

'Oh great. Maybe we'll pinch ourselves a poacher.'

We drove through and refastened the gate. Here the track was descending through a belt of elms. At the foot of the descent lay a wash of mud, and in the mud was a clear imprint of tyres.

'Is your poacher mechanized?'

'Yeah, well,' Hanson said. 'It could be the farmer has business down here.'

'Park the car,' I told the D.C. 'Perhaps we need a walk to clear our brains.'

We left the car. Now the track climbed again, with the elms still tall on either hand; but then it levelled suddenly and made a shallow turn; and there, at the turn, stood a blue Viva.

'Hell!' Hanson breathed.

We hastened up to it. It was unlocked, and the keys were missing. It carried a West Essex registration, and the licence had been issued in Harlow. In the glove compartment were maps, pressure-gauge, duster and service records from a Harlow garage. They were made out to K. Stillwell, Orchard Croft, Harlow. The driving seat was pushed back. The boot was locked.

'Pinched,' Hanson said.

'If it's Bilney's.'

'Yeah, but it has to be,' Hanson snapped. He hoisted the bonnet, popped open the distributor and dropped the rotor arm in his pocket. 'So now he won't be travelling far, and all we have to do is grab him.'

'Unless he has pinched another car.'

'Oh sure, they grow on trees out this way.'

He bustled away up the track: I signalled the others to follow. A hundred yards further on the belt of elms ceased abruptly. Beyond lay a slope of shaggy pasture, running down to reed-beds and a weed-choked pool; but to the right, nestling under the trees, stood a timber chalet and a cluster of sheds. Seeing it, Hanson broke into a run, and there seemed little point in bawling to him to wait. We raced after him. Breckles had the good sense to shepherd the D.C. to the rear of the chalet. Hanson vaulted the rail of a verandah which enclosed the front of the building and launched his shoulder at the door. But the door didn't give.

Hanson thumped it. 'Come out, Bilney. We've got your hidey-hole surrounded!'

No response. Hanson thumped again; then ran to a window and peered in through his hands.

'Jesus Christ!'

He backed away from the window, his lantern-jaw sagging. I jumped up beside him.

'What's the matter?'

'There's a bleeding body in there!'

CHAPTER FOURTEEN

THE D.C. FETCHED a tool-roll from the car and Breckles expertly jemmied the door. The body was in a room to the right of a hall that extended from the front of the chalet to the kitchen. The room was a bedroom; it was sparsely furnished with a Safari camp bed and a folding chair; the body was lying beside the bed on the side that was furthest from the door. It lay on its back. The arms were bent, the fingers hooked, the legs folded sideways. It was terrifyingly dead: wide-eyed and snarling. There was a lot of blood on the board floor.

Hanson sent air hissing through his teeth. 'Hell oh hell. The bloody bastard.'

Breckles and the D.C. were staring pop-eyed; most likely they hadn't seen a killing before.

'Is this — is he the chummie?' Breckles ventured.

Somehow that horror defied identification. The face was now the simple face of humanity, shocked and outraged by a hideous dying. But there was the blunt finger, clawing at air.

I nodded. 'He's Bilney.'

'But who . . . what happened?'

I hunched a shoulder. 'Someone stabbed him. Can't you see?'

Perhaps Breckles couldn't see. Bilney's shirt-front looked just a chewed-up, bloody mess. I kicked the bed aside and approached the body, taking care to keep my shoes from the blood. There were multiple stab-wounds in thorax and abdomen, defensive cuts on each hand. Bilney had fought, but it hadn't helped him. The attack had been too strong, too fierce. It had ended in a frenzy of superfluous stabbing as Bilney lay dying beside the bed. When? I stooped to manipulate a leg; rigor mortis was complete. The blood-puddle was largely congealed, though still liquid towards the centre. Sometime yesterday: perhaps mid-afternoon, when Bilney had returned from his rendezvous with Deslauriers. The killer had been waiting for him: he may have suspected it, have left his car down the track while he reconnoitred.

But now . . . what?

One killer, or two?

This time there was no clue of sinistrality. Just a knife going in with mortal hatred: someone who couldn't kill Bilney enough.

I fished for his wallet, a smart lizard-skin number. Like Freddy's wallet, it hadn't been robbed. Forty-seven pounds in fives and ones, a twice-endorsed driving licence, stamps, receipts. A revenge kill-ing? One for one? But somebody had known where to look for Bilney. Had tracked him to this obscure place: maybe with a little help from his friends.

I stood back from the body and looked round the

room, but the room was emptier than a punishment cell. The chair, the camp-bed, the naked floor: boards of which creaked under my foot. I stooped to finger one. It pulled up easily, the securing nails rusted through. Underneath, an empty air-space and the puggy smell of dry-rot. A futile gesture. I dropped the board back. All that room really contained was the body.

'Come on. There has to be a phone here somewhere.'

'Yeah, but it doesn't make bloody sense!' Hanson yapped.

'It made sense to someone,' I said. 'And he was no playboy. This chummie we need behind bars.'

'But who'd want to do it?'

I stamped down the board. 'Perhaps who wanted it done is a better question. Only standing here won't get any answers, so let's call in the people who may have some.'

Nobody was sorry to get out of the bedroom. We found the phone, as I knew we would. This was clearly where Bilney had spent his time during his absences from the Reed-Cutters. No doubt he had jibbed at staying at a place that was so remote and uncomfortably furnished; but here was his point of contact, and here each day he would have to come. In fact, we found the evidence by the phone: a chair and a tin-lid of cigarette-ends. Sitting there, he would have been told of Freddy's appointment with Rampant, would have received his summons to meet Deslauriers . . .

I left Hanson to do the phoning and joined the others in a search of the premises. What the theory of a killer waiting in ambush needed was evidence of a

142

break-in, and that we found in a forced window. But not very much else. In the bleak little kitchen was a cache of empty cans and soiled picnic plates; half a sliced loaf, a lump of cheese, tea, sugar and tinned milk. In the Elsan closet we found a local paper with Freddy's demise in the stop-press, and outside a few spots of oil showing where Bilney had parked the Viva.

When we returned to the parlour we found Hanson seated by the phone with an inspired light in his grey eye. He had a cheroot going; he waved it at us, adding ash of his to ash of Bilney's.

'Sit down. I've got the whole picture.'

There was only one other chair: I took it.

'Look, I've been thinking about what you said. It's not who did it, but who wanted it done.'

'I said that might be the angle.'

'But yeah. It fits all down the line. From somebody shopping Freddy's mob to us finding chummie behind the what-not.'

I shrugged, guessing pretty well what was coming. That notion had jumped into my mind, too. But there were snags. It wasn't nearly as simple as Hanson was now proposing to make it seem.

'Let's have it, then.'

'It's like this. We've got it all happening round Deslauriers. Nothing goes on but she has a link with it. Unless she's in the middle, it doesn't work.'

I nodded. 'Go on.'

'Take it back to the beginning. Freddy coming up here to do a job. It goes like clockwork, but surprise, surprise – someone blows the gaff to Met.'

'You can take it back further,' I said.

143

'How's that?'

'Someone influenced Freddy to do that job. It wasn't in his class. Below a hundred grand, Freddy wouldn't have wasted a week in the country.'

Hanson paused. 'You're saying she persuaded him?'

I trailed my hand. 'You're telling me.'

'Yeah, well, why not? He was loopy over her. If she said jump, he'd fall off a cliff.' He fizzed smoke. 'So take it all the way: she had this caper planned from the start. A job out of London with a hideaway handy, where the killer can wait till she turns him on. And that's how it worked out. The mob pulled the robbery, Deslauriers arranged for Met to be waiting. Because why? Because the mob might make her trouble if they got the idea she'd bumped-off Freddy. Are you happy with that?'

'Who phoned in the tip-off?'

'What's wrong with chummie next door?'

'He'd be in London.'

'Who says she didn't phone him?'

I nodded reluctantly: it was possible.

'Fine,' Hanson said. 'That was the mob fixed. Now she could whistle up her killer. He picked himself a nice car and arrived in Haughton Thursday evening. But the lady didn't like him staying in the open so she sent him on here. Only this place is damp or it has draughts, so chummie took a room at a cosy pub.'

'Hold it,' I said. 'I don't like that part.'

'Huh?' Hanson's thick brows registered surprise.

'If Deslauriers had planned this, Bilney wouldn't have gone to Haughton and taken the risk of meeting her at the Barge-House.'

Hanson dragged on the cheroot. 'But that's what happened.'

'That's what happened, and it doesn't fit. Bilney should have been briefed to come straight out here, and not to have shown in Haughton at all.'

'Perhaps he lost his way, sir,' Breckles suggested. 'A stranger wouldn't find Turnpudden Hole in a hurry.'

'Yeah,' Hanson said. 'Yeah, that has to be it. He lost his way and had to get instructions.' He gave me a leer. 'Okay?'

'He didn't need to book a room to get instructions.'

'So he was fed up with horsing around. And that makes sense to me, anyway.'

He stared around, daring comment. I let it go. Hanson dragged smoke.

'Now we have him sitting by this phone. Rampant made his play for Freddy. Deslauriers saw it as an opportunity, got on the blower and alerted Bilney. Deslauriers knew where the meeting would take place because Freddy described it to her from last time. Bilney was waiting when Freddy turned up and he came in behind and let him have it. So that was part two over. The mob was inside, Freddy was cooling on the heath. What should have happened next was Bilney going home and leaving the coppers to chase their arses. Only Bilney doesn't do that. And why not? Because he's caught the sweet smell of money. If Deslauriers wanted Freddy dead the odds are she stands to collect his dough. So Bilney stays and acts tough, and Deslauriers has to get him off her back.' He drew breath. 'What's your guess at the E.T.D.?'

'Near enough to the time you're after.'

'Three or four p.m.?'

'About that. I'm not a professional, but I've watched them at work.'

'And that would be the time you met Deslauriers yesterday? When she was moored at this end of the Broad?'

I nodded. 'All that part fits. Deslauriers could have been setting him up.'

'So that's it,' Hanson said. 'What we're looking at in there is part three. Bilney tried too hard, and the lady countered with another rough boy from the Smoke. And this time I'll bet it was a quick, smart job, with chummie taking off for home straight afterwards. Which is where we'll find him, if we find him. This end the case has gone cold.'

He shot me a fierce look, backed with smoke.

'It does seem to make sense, sir,' Breckles ventured.

'Of course it does,' Hanson snorted. 'Deslauriers has to be the one behind it.'

I wriggled a shoulder. 'I give you that. Deslauriers is in it up to her neck. But there is one thing that goes on bothering me about this phenomenal eruption of pro killers.'

'And what's that?'

'The level of ferocity.'

'Huh?'

'We've just been looking at another example. And it's like the first: too many blows struck. In fact, too like the first for comfort.'

Hanson, about to jump in, checked himself. 'Are you trying to tell me it's the one man?'

I nodded. 'I think it has to be. And that one man

is no pro. He's an amateur, probably a psychopath, paranoid, his temper on a hair-trigger. A hate-killer. A man with grudges against both Bilney and Freddy.'

Hanson stared, his eyes rimmed. 'Oh, come on now! What's his motive?'

'At a guess, I'd say Madame Deslauriers. As you were saying, she must be behind it.'

Hanson did his famous impression of a man watching a giraffe turn into an elephant: then he came down on the tin-lid with his cheroot stub and mashed the stub into shreds.

'It won't work!'

I shrugged. 'It will. It fits the evidence better than the other way.'

'Like hell it does. Just ask yourself this — why was Bilney here, if not to do Freddy?'

'He would be here because he was sweet on Deslauriers.'

Hanson hooted. 'That's so likely! And him leaving a note in his pad to tell his girl-friend he was on a job.'

'It's the sort of note he might have left a girl-friend. No doubt he would still have uses for Mavis. And the note troubles me a good deal less than Bilney's turning up at Haughton unannounced.'

'Yeah, yeah,' Hanson said. 'Big point taken. And the mob getting shopped — how about that?'

'Call it part of the same deal. Malice towards Freddy. Followed by a knife when opportunity offered.'

Hanson threw up his hands. 'It stinks. And all this time the lady sits by smiling.'

'She may not know, or not know all of it. Then she would behave in just the way she's behaving.'

'It still stinks.'

'Listen,' I said. 'Let's give it a run-through my way. The evidence points to the sort of killer I've described. At least we have to try it from that view-point.'

Hanson clawed his hand across his face. 'Okay, you try it.'

'First we know that Bilney was acquainted with Wicken. Deslauriers admits that she has met all the gang, and so through Wicken she could have met Bilney. It doesn't have to follow that Bilney was her boy-friend, but it could very well follow that he was attracted by her. If he learned from Wicken that she was staying at Haughton he might have been foolish enough to come out after her.'

'Him having such a sentimental record,' Hanson said sourly.

'Perhaps. But the lady has a lot of horse-power. And it squares with Bilney taking a room at the Three Tuns and bribing a waiter to smuggle her a message. A paid killer wouldn't have run those risks, but they would be part of the fun for a roughneck Romeo. And Deslauriers was game. She didn't want him next door, but he was welcome to stay around to brighten up the scenery.'

Hanson sniffed. 'Yeah, that sounds like her. A lover boy in every bush.'

'So she sent him here, where he could nurse the phone and be available for romps. Bilney didn't fancy sleeping here, but he wasn't hiding, so there was no reason why he should. Even Freddy's murder probably didn't worry him, and may have given him a motive for staying on. Now he was free from competition and could expect a readier response from Deslauriers.'

'It's lovely,' Hanson said. 'I'm almost sold. But then why does Bilney finish up so dead?'

'For the same reason that Freddy did,' I said. 'They were both Deslauriers' lovers.'

'You mean there's a mad lover in the scene somewhere?'

'For the moment I'm merely reading the evidence. It suggests that Bilney didn't come here as a paid killer, but that it was his connection with Deslauriers that led to his death.'

Hanson glared at Breckles. 'Which side are you on?'

Breckles looked flustered and rolled his shoulders.

'Me too,' Hanson said. 'It's a way of looking at it, but I always gag at demon lovers.'

'And the mode of the killings?'

'I'll swallow them,' Hanson said. 'What's wrong with some pro killings being messy? Bilney's job may have been his first, and what happened here a tit for tat.'

'That was never a pro job.'

'You're forgetting who paid for it. The lady could have ordered fancy trimmings. And I would sooner go along with that than with a leching Bilney and a demon lover.' He hesitated, eyes suddenly small. 'Or did you have a candidate in mind?'

I let my face go blank. 'Just someone in the know. Who is left-handed.'

CHAPTER FIFTEEN

A N AMBULANCE AND two Wolseleys came up the track and halted smartly where Bilney had been parking the Viva. Hanson strutted out to take command, I strolled away down the rough meadow.

Down there by the pool was a different world from the shabby chalet with its busy policemen. All fresh growth, thrusting new reeds, tender-leaved alders and polleny willows. Water-hens foraged among the rushes; a handsome male grebe fished the open water; reed-warblers flirted among last-year's reeds and made creaky, dripping comments. A world that couldn't care less about the mind-ridden animals up the slope: the perverted, self-doomed animals who killed each other when they weren't hungry.

I lit my pipe and continued to stroll, switching my mind off for later. I came to an old, ruinous hide, sited to overlook the pool and the reed-beds. A trace of Clytie Gifford, no doubt. I squatted for some minutes on its crude bench. The grebe came close, and I spotted its mate seated haughtily on their sloppy nest. Then a true breath-catcher: reed-pheasants: two pairs, swinging musically through the fawn, dead stems. I sat as still as the rotting bench and let my pipe go cold in my mouth.

What a hell of a place for Bilney to have come to: a hell of a place for him to die in!

The pool, the lodging, were for gentle people, gentle as the birds and the tranquil trees.

Yet here he had come, loutish, insensible, locked in some grubby prison of intent: basely living and basely dying, with his sneering eyes staring blind.

What did he want? What did any of them want?

There was nothing they were capable of receiving.

In or out of the Scrubs, the Moor, they were prisoners, the key turned by their own hand.

I got up angrily, disturbing the reed-pheasants and sending the grebe into an instant dive. I stamped back to the chalet, and stood watching policemen puffing their powder and flashing cameras.

Two hours later they were through, and the corpse had already departed for town. The results were debatable, due very largely to the unhelpful character of the chalet. It was a bad place for dabs. The paintwork was rough and the metalwork corroded. Whether chummie had been careful with his break-in or not, there were no traces of latents round the forced window. Even Bilney's dabs were found only once, some faint impressions on the bedroom door. And in the kitchen, and again in the Viva, were slight indications that wiping had taken place.

Hanson received this intelligence with gloomy satisfaction.

'At least it proves one thing – chummie was a pro.'

I couldn't contradict that. My enthusiastic amateur would scarcely have bothered with such refinements.

'But what was he doing in Bilney's car?'

Hanson flipped his hand. 'Seeing what he could nick. There was a car with no owner. Chummie just couldn't help giving it a frisk.'

'He didn't rob the body.'

'Maybe he was squeamish.'

'I'm told the knife went in eleven times.'

'Yeah, well.' Hanson squirmed. 'Then there'd be blood about, wouldn't there? He wouldn't be keen to get mixed up with that.'

I shrugged and didn't push the point; yet still it seemed a little odd. Chummie had finished his job and was on his way out, then he stopped to enter the blue Viva. Something obvious that took his eye? A clue that might have led us to him? Ah well: we would know one day, or know we didn't need to know.

I drove back to the Norchester H.Q. with Hanson and put through a call to Dainty. I got his assistant, Inspector Jason, a dapper young man with a cooing accent. Jason had no news for me. I told him my news; he listened with little dove-like murmurs. He liked the bit about the multiple stab-wounds and the blood pooled round the body.

'Do you have a sus, sir?'

'Not exactly a sus. There are two schools of thought going here. One says the killer is a pro from town. That's the school you had better follow.'

'The Super is betting on Whitey Ferrier, sir. We've had whispers from the snouts. Quarles set up a snatch for Ferrier last month and the job went sour. We made three arrests.'

'Great,' I said. 'Great. But now we want whispers about a hard boy. He would certainly have been missing from the scene all yesterday. He uses a knife, and he's far from stupid. Are you taking notes?'

'Wait – yes, sir!'

'Here is the thing that may catch him. He has probably had connections with the Quarles gang: enough so that Deslauriers would know how to contact him.'

'Is she your sus for setting it up, sir?'

'She's my nothing. Just get me some action.'

Jason cooed assurances, and I hung up. Hanson, who'd been listening, fingered his chin.

'I'd say the lady was our next move,' he said. 'Maybe we could spare her some photographs of Bilney.'

I rocked my chair and gazed over his head. 'Would you have finished with Freddy's car?'

'What's that got to do with it?'

'She wants it back. And letting her have it would be a nice gesture.'

He was gazing hard at me. 'You want us to give it to her?'

I twitched a shoulder. 'It's been in my mind. Wondering what she intends to do with it. Who'll be sitting behind the wheel.'

'You mean she's planning a skip?'

'I don't know that. But just now she lacks the number one requisite.'

Hanson rasped his chin again.

Five minutes later, I was sitting in the Bugatti.

★ ★ ★

153

Or more or less in it.

One's first impression was of putting on a one-man roller-coaster: of sitting far too high and naked, and much too close to the shoulder-width wheel. The pedals were quaint but fairly available, the instrumentation on the light side; the gear-shift came to hand, though it felt grotchy, and one realized in a flash why the hand-brake was outboard. That's where the space was, not in the cockpit. The cockpit was strictly something to wear. At a guess, Louis Chiron was a short, wiry man, and his mechanic an under-nourished midget.

I started the engine and let it roll while I got used to my surroundings. Straight ahead was the curved scuttle with a half-moon windscreen mounted above it. Then a mile of curved, tapering bonnet, secured by two leather straps, and finally the geometry of the out-rigged, narrow-tyred wheels with bicycle-type mudguards curling round them. Well, it was built to drive. I clonked off the handbrake and fed in some power. Ettore's car took a bound across the M/T yard, screamed disapproval, then settled for a jerky, restive walking-pace.

We made the street. By good fortune the tea-time rush-hour was nearly over. I slanted the wheels towards the Ring Road and double-declutched cautiously through the gears. Soon we were doing a dyspeptic thirty and I was getting a bit of feel. Wind was fingering my hair and cooling the elbow I was trail-ing nonchalantly over the side. The wheel bothered me. It was giving me the impression that I had hold of the helm of the *Queen Mary*. Also the steering was surprisingly heavy, and less connected with direction than one might have supposed. I checked the brakes. In good time, they worked, though not as though they intended to waste any rubber. On the other hand the accelerator seemed set on a watch-spring, while the clutch came in like a Mills bomb.

I reached the Ring Road, where the roundabout junction taught me some more about vintage steering. It taught me also that I was driving a car that would get more consideration than any ambulance. The last hell-bent commuters stood on their noses to let Louis Chiron go through, then happily fell into procession behind him as he cantered along at the legal forty. A classless society? Not among car-owners. The same thing happened at successive roundabouts. When I came to my turn-off the queue was solid behind me, while ahead stretched a relatively empty road.

But now my moment had come. We cruised past the delimit signs. The road ahead was reasonably straight. I squeezed a little; Ettore's car pricked up its ears and began to surge. There was an Escort behind me, and for a languid moment it seemed likely to cling to my tail; then it walked backwards in the rear-view mirror and disappeared behind some trees. Small fry. Up front, an S-bend. I jigged the reluctant brakes in good time. No other traffic. I went straight through, hugging the wheel in Segrave-style. A clear road. I let her scream. The needle drifted over the ton. My hair was getting torn out by the roots, my trailed elbow was trying to flap. Bryan de Grineau should have seen this. I could feel visible slipstream shaling off me. Le Mans, Brooklands, the great days: watch me drift the next bend.

It was nearly my last. I hit it at a speed that the Lotus

would scarcely have noticed. The next moment I was doing one of those celebrated fighting-the-wheel acts straight out of a pre-war *Modern Boy*. Now I knew why they had those wheels. I was losing the rear-end in gigantic hops. At each hop the tyres gave a baleful screech and spirted distress-signals of black smoke. The real McCoy. I steered-in, steered-out for it might have been the next hundred yards, and just when it seemed it was going on for ever, the car gave a brutal lurch and came back on course. A man's car, keep it in. The tape on the wheel was sodden with sweat. I crept along at a painful sixty, waiting for the jelly to drain out of my arms.

But strangely, I felt happier after that, as though now the car and I had got to know each other. So it didn't handle like a Lotus – never mind: it still had the heart and sinew of a lion. The next firm bend I got right, putting her into it slower, coarser: a problem solved. I was learning. No doubt Chiron had had his troubles, too. We came through Wrackstead in a growling amble, nosing aside the peasant traffic. When we crossed the bridge I touched my horn: shrill trumpets blasted 'Colonel Bogey'.

I parked the Bugatti in the hotel forecourt, where it sat simmering like a contented cat. The time was between tea and dinner and the Barge-House had an unpeopled air. Dutt was in the lounge, reading an evening paper. Through the open french windows he had a view of the lawn. At the bottom of the lawn, decorating a sunbed, lounged Mimi, Madame Deslauriers.

I nodded to Dutt and took a seat by him.

'The lady looks lonely down there.'

Dutt gave me a slow grin. 'Not so lonely, sir. She's been having a teatime chat with Bavents.'

'How many does that make?'

'It makes three. She had him up in her room again this afternoon. He was in there for nearly an hour, but he didn't come out looking very chuffed.'

'Was he happier at teatime?'

'Not so as you'd notice, sir. But with all that hair it's hard to tell. My hunch is the lady wants him to do something which he isn't very keen on.'

'I'd have thought she could talk him into anything.'

'Yes, sir, you get that impression. And as a matter of fact I got round to wondering just how well they do know each other.'

I leered. 'You did, did you?'

Dutt had the grace to turn pink. 'Not like that, sir! What I mean is whether they'd met before she came here.'

A shrewd point. 'What was your conclusion?'

'Well, sir, I don't know about a conclusion. But I did give the University a tinkle to find out Bavents' home address.'

'And that was?'

'Chelsea, sir. Vought Street, Chelsea. His father keeps The Peacock pub. That's a few blocks away from Upper Cheyne Row, but not outside the lady's district.'

'Well, well,' I said. 'So they could have met.'

Dutt looked pleased. 'It's on the cards, sir. If you ask me the lady has a taste for pubs, so she could have spent an evening in The Peacock.'

'And now she wants him to do something he doesn't fancy.' I gazed down the lawn at the recumbent Mimi. She was draped elegantly in the evening sunlight, gazing at nothing through tinselly-framed sun-glasses. 'Has Bavents used the phone?'

'Not to my knowledge, sir. I've been keeping an eye on the phone.'

'Has he been out?'

'Don't think so, sir. Not since yesterday afternoon.'

I hesitated. 'He was out then?'

'Yes, sir. If you remember, I couldn't check his statement. I'd say he went out after they finished serving coffee, and it was after you came back when he returned.'

It was indeed. I did quick arithmetic. It must have taken me an hour to find Mimi's launch. In half that time Bavents could have driven to the chalet, hidden his Mini and forced the window. And Friday evening too he had been at liberty . . . while there were plenty of chef's knives in the kitchen! Dutt was eyeing me thoughtfully.

'Does that fit in, sir?'

I nodded and briefly brought him up to date. Dutt listened stolidly. I sketched Hanson's theory without bothering to throw in comment. Dutt wrinkled his nose.

'I like Bavents better, sir. Those rough boys are all for keeping it simple.'

'Where is Bavents now?'

'He's in the kitchen. Do you want me to fetch him out for you?'

I shook my head; first things first. I rose and went

down the lawn. Mimi received me with a melting smile and was gracious enough to remove her sun-glasses.

'You are back, my friend! Was the day tiresome?'

I took the Bugatti's key from my pocket. It was a custom-made, gold-plated key, attached to an enamel badge by a snake-chain. Not to be mistaken. I let it dangle. Mimi's green eyes fixed on it covetously.

'Ha! You have brought me Freddy's car.'

I gave the badge a flip. 'I've brought it from town.'

'But for me, huh?'

'Perhaps. At the moment it is just part of Freddy's estate.'

She sat up on the bed. 'But he has left it to me! You will find it is so in his will.'

'I haven't seen his will.'

'But yes, it is true! You have only to ring up Freddy's solicitors.'

I flipped the badge again. 'Of course, if you have seen it . . .'

'It is the same. I shall have the car.'

'But if I could have your word for it?'

Her eyes narrowed; she stared at the key, then back at me.

'You are mean, Monsieur. You know quite well that the car will be mine. But it doesn't matter, I will wait. Only I shall not think you are very generous.'

I moved my shoulders. 'That's too bad. Especially since I bring unpleasant news.'

'Unpleasant news? How?'

I dropped the key in my pocket. 'I think we had better talk about that in private.'

CHAPTER SIXTEEN

I GAVE DUTT the pleasure of escorting her to the office and myself went in search of Frayling. I found him in the dining-room, decanting spirit into the chef's stove from a Winchester bottle. It was near the door of the kitchen; I drew him further off.

'Did Bavents have permission to go out yesterday?'

Frayling's tentative smile became anxious. 'It was all right, wasn't it? He didn't get into any trouble?'

'Please answer the question.'

'Well – yes, I suppose so. He told me he had to attend a Student Union meeting. Apparently the meeting had been called unexpectedly and was to do with his being sent down.'

'Have you a private phone, other than in the office?'

'There's one in my flat upstairs.'

He took me there. I rang the University; I was handed around between secretaries. Eventually I contacted the Student Union liaison officer, who informed me there had been no meeting for three weeks. I asked him if Bavents' rustication was an item on their agenda, and he informed me that that was unlikely. The matter had been discussed at a previous meeting, when no motion had been put before the committee.

Frayling was concerned. 'I just don't understand it. He must have some personal problem he wants to keep quiet.'

I threw him a look. 'Don't mention this conversation to him. And don't let him out again without telling me.'

'But look – what has he done?'

'Just do as I say.'

I left him gazing after me with wretched eyes. Outside, across the road, was parked an electrician's van with two of Hanson's men yawning inside it. I went to it and slid back the door.

'Do either of you two know the waiter, Bavents?'

They didn't, so I gave them a *portrait parlé*: which in Bavents' case wasn't difficult.

'If he leaves, detain him. I want him for questioning.'

They looked uncertain. 'Will there be a charge, sir . . . ?'

'I want him stopped. Understood?'

Apparently it was. I slammed the door.

I had brought back copies of the Bilney photographs and I took them with me into the office. Mimi had appropriated the swivel chair and sat smoking, her sandalled feet on the desk. She was wearing her hot pants, along with a sleeveless top in a black, clinging jersey material; she looked politely bored, and didn't bother to glance up as I entered the room. I adjusted the curtains; Dutt, in his corner, sat quietly sharpening a pencil. I perched on a corner of the desk, remote from the sandals, and laid down the photographs with their backs uppermost.

'Have you been in a blue Viva car lately, Madame?'

Mimi considered it. She flicked ash. 'Do you think I have, Monsieur?'

'I don't know for certain. But later I shall need your fingerprint sample.'

'Aha. Then you have such a car.'

'We have both the car and the driver.'

Mimi sat still, appraising her toes. Not a twitch of emotion on her magnificent face.

'Perhaps you should ask him if I have been in his car. After all, I know nothing of the makes and colours. The cars today are so much the same. It is only the men that one remembers.'

'Unfortunately, this driver is answering no questions.'

'No?' The corners of her mouth dimpled. 'Possibly he is nervous, being questioned by policemen. I believe it happens with many people.'

'I am sure he isn't nervous.'

'Then it may be stubborn? In some subtle way you have hurt his feelings?'

'This man doesn't have feelings, Madame Deslauriers. I have pictures of him here. Would you care to see them?'

Her eyes flickered to mine. She could sense a trap, but there was now no way for her to avoid it; and doubtless she felt confident she could control herself and subdue any sign of recognition. She reached for the top photograph and turned it over.

Her cry had the thrill of mortal agony.

Her legs jerked from the desk: she sprang up, gasping, and stood with her face turned to the wall. She hugged herself, her breasts, her stomach, fighting to hold her hysteria in check. The sense of violence was awesome. She should have fainted; instead, there was this brief, epileptic-like struggle; then the frantic breathing began to subside, and her arms sank shakily to her sides. She pulled round to face me again, her cheeks flushed, her eyes smouldering.

'You . . . *pig*!'

I reached for the photograph, but she lunged forward and seized it with eager greed. She gazed at it angrily, triumphantly. Then she threw it in my face.

'That was cheap, you pig – cheap! How dare you show me such a picture?'

I returned the photograph to the pile. 'I certainly agree it should not have been necessary.'

'You take advantage. That is how my husband died. It is what they did to poor Freddy. You say "Aha, aha, this will break her down. This is just the thing for little Mimi".'

'You are over-reacting, Madame.'

'Pig!'

'You were less disturbed when the victim was Freddy.'

'Did I see such photographs of what happened there? Were they pushed under my nose in this fashion?'

'Freddy was your lover.'

'Ha, ha, lover! In the end we were just friends.'

'You had no grief for him. Surely this emotion is excessive for a mere stranger?'

'It is not for a stranger. It is for shock. It is for that horror you make me see. It is unfair, a low trick. I am angry: I despise you.'

I shook my head. 'Too uncharacteristic.'

'Ha?'

'Madame Deslauriers has more poise.'

'Beast and pig!'

'I think Madame Deslauriers could have seen that picture without turning a hair.'

'Am I a butcher then? An executioner?'

'You are a person of coolness and resource.'

'Ha-ha, flattery will not do either.'

'Nor will any further denial that you know that man.'

She snatched her head and glared at the pile of photographs. Her colour had slowly been returning to normal. Her breathing was well in check again and her hands trailing loose. Now she let her eyes die, too, the lids relaxing and hooding. The passionate set of her lips began to soften, to curve.

'You are a bastard, Monsieur. Which you know very well.'

'Perhaps you will take your seat again.'

'But understand that I hate you.'

She sat however, and replaced her immaculate feet on the desk. Then she took cigarettes from her pants-pocket, lit one and blew caressing smoke.

'Of course, I do know that man. I knew him when you showed me the picture this morning. But I did not choose to acknowledge that. Which you will admit is my privilege.'

'Why didn't you choose to acknowledge it?'

164

She cocked a shoulder. 'Let us say you were interrupting my breakfast. Also I did not know him well. I didn't wish to answer questions.'

'You know his name?'

'Why not? Bilney.'

'How did you come to make his acquaintance?'

'One evening I was in the Hammersmith Feathers with Freddy and Wicken and we were joined by this man. We went on to other pubs. He came with us. I think he was hoping for some business with Freddy. There were plenty of hangers-on like that. Doing a job for Freddy was a safe thing.'

'Did Freddy employ him?'

'You must ask Wicken. It was he who introduced him to Freddy.'

'But after that you would see him around again?'

'Oh no. I saw him just that once. He was not my style, you understand. He was a dull-witted, uncouth boy. If you ask me I do not think Freddy would have used him. Freddy was a man who required intelligence.'

'But he was a friend of Wicken's. And Wicken you did see.'

'Wickey, yes. Not Wickey's friends.'

'So you could have got in touch with Bilney through Wicken.'

'I suppose I could. But why should I?'

'Say a personal interest.'

She laughed derisively. 'I tell you already he is not my style. I like some subtlety with my beef. Even among policemen one can find it.'

'Then what about Bilney?'

'What about him?'

'Didn't Bilney take a personal interest in you?'

She gestured with the cigarette. 'He was lecherous, of course. But it goes no further with that sort of animal.'

'He didn't try to see you?'

'I think you are joking.'

'Didn't follow you around? Angle for attention?'

'Not that one. Never.'

'Yet we find him in Haughton. Staying next door. Sending you a message.'

She breathed out a long miasma of smoke. 'Does that make sense to you, my friend? That I would play footsy with such a dumb ox, when there were as good or better right on my doorstep?'

'Bilney was there. He was no mirage.'

'So. I am not responsible for that.'

'You spoke to him. Directed him to Freddy's hideaway. He could have learned of that only from you.'

'You are forgetting Wickey. Wickey would know of it.'

'Perhaps. But Bilney learned of it from you. His first move was to book at the Three Tuns. He didn't change quarters till he had talked to you.'

'I do not admit that.'

'Then tell me something else. What was Bilney's purpose in hanging around here? Sitting every day in Freddy's chalet, smoking, waiting for the phone to ring?'

She gestured peevishly. 'Why should I know this?'

'Because yesterday the phone rang, and the caller was you. You told Bilney to drive to the lane leading to the Broad, and you met him there and spent two or three hours with him.'

'I did all that?'

'You sat in the car with him. The car was pulled off into the trees. You had a picnic of sorts, fruit, chocolate – I can be more precise after the post-mortem. Because then Bilney died: straight after that. He went back to the chalet and met his killer. As though the real purpose of getting him away from the chalet had been to give the killer an opportunity for ambush.'

'And you are accusing me?'

'The killer knew where to go. He knew that Bilney would be absent. Two things that you knew and nobody else knew – just as there were two things that you knew about Freddy.'

She flicked ash on the floor. 'Poor Mimi. This is quite a formidable indictment.'

'I think you had better help us.'

'That was always inevitable. You are a man of such persuasion, my friend.'

She wanted a drink, but I wouldn't permit it; she sat awhile with a sulky expression. Though I had drawn the curtains of the door and counter windows, we could hear chattering people passing along to the dining-room. The sound accentuated the arrest of time which is the peculiar quality of interrogation. My refusing the drink had been a symbol. Now we were remote from the world of innocence.

At last she folded her legs with a sigh.

'Monsieur's psychology is impeccable. I am a

creature exposed to perpetual temptation. How sad if I spent my time rejecting it.'

'Bilney was your lover?'

She made a faint mouth. 'I would rather not award him that title. He was – what shall we say? – a taste for garlic. He served as a purge for the coarser emotions.'

'How long was he put to these medicinal uses?'

'Oh, he has been around since Easter. I met him as I told you, in the Hammersmith Feathers. Next day he rang me. It developed from there.'

'Did you go to his flat?'

She hesitated. 'No. There is a discreet hotel in Kensington. Not that we used it very often. One takes purges only occasionally.'

'He was keen?'

'Naturally.'

'Wanted more than you would give him?'

'Yes. It is the character of the type. Because of that we had a disagreement, which is why he followed me up here.'

'What was he trying for?'

Her hand lifted. 'Some more artichokes on the same basis He was stupid, but not so stupid as to suppose I would leave Freddy. Of course, I wouldn't let him stay in Haughton, but I was tickled to think he had come after me. So I told him he would have to lie low in the chalet, and perhaps I would ring him, perhaps I wouldn't.'

'And he settled for that?'

'He was sure I would ring him. And he may not have been entirely wrong. It was dull here; Freddy was boring. I think Bilney may have gone to bat.'

I nodded. It was fitting pretty well; I could believe in Bilney playing along. He had tasted the honey and it was some honey: worth a little patience for another dip.

But that had been Thursday.

'How often did you ring him?'

'I gave him a call every day. It was amusing, like teasing a pet. He tried lots of tricks to make me say yes.'

'When on Friday?'

'You know when. My famous call to the theatre.'

'After Rampant's call.'

'I do not deny it. But I said nothing of that matter to Bilney.'

She faced me with frank eyes; it was either true or cleverly untrue. By freely conceding a critical point she was leaving me no room for manoeuvre. And alas, she was skilful enough to have done that. I could read nothing from her eyes. A frank look is a frank look, besides being the hallmark of accomplished liars.

'Wouldn't Freddy's absence have given you a chance to meet Bilney?'

'Ha-ha, do you think I lacked chances? I was not married to Freddy, you know. I do not recognize a monopoly.'

'Still, you would have looked for a discreet occasion?'

'Any day I could take a launch down the river. No, no, I wasn't giving it to Bilney so easily. A little waiting would improve his manners, ha?'

'But you did know Freddy would be out when you rang him.'

'I have told you, yes. I knew when and where. But I did not tell Bilney. It was not his business. It would have encouraged him to come here, and I didn't want that.'

Another frank stare, with a flash of indignation.

'Very well then. You rang, but you didn't tell him. The next day you learned what had happened to Freddy. Wasn't it risky to let Bilney hang around after that?'

She threw up her hands. 'Are you telling me! It was more than risky, it was suicidal. With the police running about spending the tax-payers' money and looking for just such a boy as little Bilney. But he wouldn't go. He thought now was his chance. No longer did Mimi have to hoodwink her Freddy. He was more than stupid, he was mad. I do not wonder he finished up like this.'

'Did you see him?'

'No! Do you think I am mad too? I could scarcely push past the police to the telephone. It was not till yesterday that they went away, that I could arrange to give Bilney a lecture.'

'That was your object yesterday?'

'What else?'

'You seem to have spent several hours with Bilney.'

'Because he is an imbecile! It was like drilling concrete. Surely you have met these cretins before?'

'So the picnic was fortuitous.'

'It was food that he brought. He has not been living on fresh air. And I got hungry talking to the ape. I didn't expect it would take me so long.'

'And what was the result?'

'Not any result. He would not promise to go away.'

'But after so much oratory? Three hours?'

'Pyuh!' It was a noise like a cat's.

I let my eyes drift, then snapped them back suddenly. 'Tell me, Mimi. Who killed Bilney?'

Her eyes were steady. 'Someone with a knife.'

'His name.'

Her eyes mocked me. 'Why should I tell you?'

I got up and walked over to the window. The Bugatti was sitting proudly where I had parked it. Across the way lurked the tradesman's van and the shadowy faces of the two D.C.'s. Some traffic was crawling across the junction, but the road in front of me was empty; sunlight was slanting on the bank opposite and lighting the windows of a flat built above it. I watched it as I talked.

'Listen carefully. You've told me too much and too little. You have admitted sending Bilney to the chalet and calling him out to a meeting yesterday. We are back where we began. You knew he was there. You knew he would be absent for several hours. They are two things which only you knew. You must also know who killed Bilney.'

She gave a little low chuckle. 'A logical Englishman. And I thought you trusted only the intuition.'

I turned from the window. 'I need a logical answer. Or you may be spending tonight in a cell.'

'Aha, a threat.' She leaned back in her chair and hooked her thumbs in the sleeveless top. 'Yet the cells are no strange thing to me, my friend. And I am told they are better furnished over here.' She lowered her lids with their perfect lashes. 'So then. Let us ventilate your logic. Would it be surprising if the man who killed Freddy was also the man who killed Bilney?'

I said nothing. She nodded emphatically.

'Oh yes. Oh yes. The same man. You show me the photograph. It is done with a knife. Unhappily, I know about these things. So, one man. He has killed Freddy. He is perhaps not a stranger in this district. He doesn't go away. He is here, watching. He has seen Bilney. He has tracked him home. Then, where is the difficulty? He wishes to kill Bilney, decides he will lay for him in the chalet. Now he watches till Bilney goes away, which by chance is to meet me.' She held out her hand. 'Is this impossible? Does it not fit the facts as well? Would a jury prefer your version to mine? And so bang goes your logic.'

'Not quite,' I said. 'There is a matter of motive.'

'Oh, motive! That is for counsels.'

'In this case a motive of massive gain. Freddy had more to leave than the Bugatti.'

Her eyes widened. 'You have seen the will?'

I nodded. 'And so, I suspect, have you.'

'You are wrong, my friend.'

'It amounts to the same thing. Freddy's whole estate is willed to you.'

'This is true?'

'Yes.'

She looked away. There was a sparkle between her lashes. 'But how sad. I didn't need it, and he was just going to enjoy his life.'

I watched her hungrily. They were real tears; if it was an act it had the stamp of sincerity. I didn't think

172

it was an act. She wasn't giving it enough emphasis. From where he was sitting, Dutt probably couldn't see it.

'All the same, it leaves you the gainer.'

She twisted her mouth. 'Does that make me guilty?'

'It will weigh with juries.'

'We have not come to juries. We have not come to anything but so-called logic.'

'Then we will follow that. How long have you known Bavents?'

She was silent for a moment, still looking away from me.

'What makes you ask that?'

'A piece of information. Bavents' father keeps a pub in Vought Street, Chelsea.'

'Aha. The Peacock.' She gestured wearily. 'All right. I admit it. I know the yak. But he is not my lover, has not been my lover. Even with me such things are possible.'

'He was in your room twice today.'

'So then. I have to talk to someone.'

'Once for an hour.'

'It was a longer talk.'

'And again at tea, on the lawn.'

She tossed her hair irritably. 'What is all this about? I find the yak an interesting subject. He is full of fire, full of passion. Simply he dare not say boo.'

'You were merely teasing him?'

'Not merely, my friend. Teasing a man is a great art. He must always be having a little hope, a belief that his reward will come in the end.'

'And that was Bavents' situation?'

'Every man's. What do you think a woman is made of?'

'But Bavents is infatuated.'

She kissed a finger. 'At his age, surely it does no harm.'

I stared into her eyes. 'Only that is what I'm wondering. Whether it couldn't do him a great deal of harm. Whether it couldn't lead him into some fantasy world where right and wrong are not clearly defined.'

She pouted. 'You are not serious?'

'Very serious. His record doesn't suggest a stable character.'

'But Monsieur, I have just amused myself.'

'No more than that?'

She wriggled and tossed her hair again.

'What were you wanting him to do today?'

She checked fractionally. 'Who says I did?'

'You had long talks with him. He was reluctant. You were perhaps pushing him too far.'

'Huh.' She made a sweep with her hand. 'Now it is you who are fantastical, Monsieur. He is a moody yak, that is all. I think you had better stick to logic.'

'Is that all you are telling me?'

'Isn't it enough?'

I came off the desk suddenly and stepped to the door. I threw it open and stood beside it. She watched me with an expression of mocking surprise.

'It is time to go?'

I held the door and said nothing. She rose disdainfully and marched from the office. I slammed down in the swivel-chair and lit my pipe. I jerked a hand to Dutt.

'Fetch Bavents.'

CHAPTER SEVENTEEN

THERE WAS A delay, probably occasioned by Frayling's reluctance to lose Bavents during dinner; then he arrived, hot-faced and nervous, with Dutt nudging him from behind. I pointed to a chair. Bavents sat or sprawled; his blushing hands clutched his knees. He was either sweatily, meltingly innocent, or aware that a point of no return was fast being reached. I tried to fix his staring eye.

'Madame Deslauriers has just been helping us. She says she was acquainted with you in Chelsea and she admits to several recent conversations. Now I am going to ask you a frank question, and I would like you carefully to consider your reply.'

His eyes rolled; his body was trembling.

'Did you kill Frederick Quarles and Thomas Bilney?'

His mouth worked and he made a gulping sound; the flush ebbed suddenly from his cheeks.

'Did you?'

'N-n-no! I didn't!'

'It would be best to get it over now.'

'P-please, no!'

'It will save you some distress.'

'B–but I didn't. I didn't!'

'Think carefully.'

'No!'

I checked. He was swaying dangerously, teetering on the rim of a faint. Push him some more, and he would go over; he wasn't ready to confess yet. I swung in the swivel-chair.

'Very well then. Perhaps you can help us in other ways. We know now you took a message from Bilney to Madame Deslauriers. Were you in the yard when she came out?'

'I was w-working on my car—'

'And you returned to it after you had taken in the message?'

'Well, y–yes. But I didn't hear anything. They went over behind the garages.'

'You saw them meet?'

'Yes.'

'Would you say they seemed fond of each other?'

The flush began again. 'He kissed her. She was worrying about him being seen.'

'But she was fond of him too?'

'Well, I'd s–say so.'

'In fact, they met like two lovers?'

Bavents chewed his lip. 'Yes, I suppose so. But she w–wasn't so keen on him as he was on her.'

'How long were they talking?'

He dragged at his knees. 'About quarter of an hour, twenty minutes.'

'But you heard nothing of it.'

'No! Why should I l-listen to what they were saying?'

'That's fairly obvious. You would be jealous.'

'I wasn't jealous and I wasn't listening!'

'You just went back to tinkering with your engine. While she was in his arms behind the garages.'

He punished the knees. 'I d-didn't want to listen! I made a lot of noise revving the engine. When they came out she said something about ringing him, that's all I heard. Then she went in.'

'What was wrong with your engine?'

'The s-slow-running is dicey—'

'Skip it,' I said. 'Now tell me about Friday.'

He licked his lips with small conviction. 'I d-don't know anything about Friday. I didn't see Mr Quarles except at meal-times. I think he spent a lot of time in his room.'

'Which I am told is next door to yours.'

'I can't help that! I didn't see him.'

'But you could have heard him. Heard him discussing a certain matter with Madame Deslauriers.'

'No! It isn't true.'

'It could easily be true. You are not particular about loafing near doors. And if Quarles was excited and raising his voice you could very likely have heard him through the wall. Wasn't that what happened?'

'No, it wasn't!'

'Where were you in the evening?'

'I was here – in the hotel—'

'On your evening off?'

His eyes popped at me.

'You had time and opportunity,' I said. 'You could

very well have known where Quarles was going. And I daresay what you heard going on in the next room was motive enough for wanting him away. At least you could stop that. There were knives in the kitchen. All you had to do was follow in your Mini. If you want me to believe different you'll need to come up with something pretty convincing.'

'But I was here – in my room!'

'Your room is no alibi.'

'Yes, but I w-was. Ask Mimi!'

'Madame Deslauriers was with you?'

'Yes – no!' He clawed his hands together desperately. 'She could have heard me m-moving about. She was in her room too, she might remember.'

'I'll certainly ask her,' I said.

Bavents groaned and wrestled his hands.

I gave my chair another swing. 'Next, you would want to settle Bilney.'

Bavents shuddered.

'To make time for that you had to fake an excuse to Mr Frayling.'

'But I didn't go there!'

I hesitated. 'Where?'

He gasped as though I'd punched him in the wind.

'Look, I was in Norchester! It's true, I was! I just had to go into town yesterday.'

'So you weren't where?'

'Not anywhere! I had to meet a m-man in Norchester.'

'What man?'

'This man—'

'*What man?*'

'He – I d–don't know what his name is!'

'Just a man with no name.'

'Yes! No name! You meet him in the shelter in Chapel Field Gardens.' He was breathing jerkily, his colour draining. 'Ask any student, they'll t-tell you!'

'Do you mean he's a pusher?'

Bavents nodded.

I rose. 'Come on. We'll take a look in your room.'

The pot was there: about half an ounce of it, packed in an OHMS envelope. Also five crudely-rolled joints and the butt-ends of two more. We searched the room. It was a tiny place with a slanted roof and a dormer window; bare space for a bed, a chair, a chest-of-drawers and a hanging wardrobe behind the door. Books were piled on the chest-of-drawers, mostly works on politics and economics, and on the chair were four or five notebooks, filled with neat, small writing. Bavents didn't interfere. He stood out in the passage, watching us through the open door. Apart from the pot we found nothing. I tapped the dividing-wall: it was lath-and-plaster.

'You say you bought this stuff yesterday?'

Bavents shrugged his narrow shoulders.

'Can you prove that?'

'There's the m-man—'

'Forget it. The pusher won't be giving evidence.' I took the pot and squeezed out of the room. 'Now. I'm going to charge you with possession. You had better pack a few things in a case, because you won't be coming back here tonight.'

'You're going to charge me with p-possession?'

'Does this look like a plant?'

He stared for some moments through his mane. Then he turned into the room, in a beaten sort of way, and began stuffing toilet gear in a zip-bag.

I left him in Dutt's charge while I went to ring Hanson and to order a car. In the hall I intercepted Madame Deslauriers on her way to dinner, dressed now in her slinky, slit-skirt gown.

'Just a moment.'

'Please, Monsieur. You have made me late already.'

'This won't take long. It's about Friday evening. You told us you retired to your room after dinner.'

'So?'

'Did you order up any drinks?'

'Yes. You may confirm that with the waiter.'

'Bavents?'

She smiled insolently. 'No. It was the German boy, Fritz.'

'Did you see or hear anything of Bavents?'

'I was watching television in my room.'

'His room is next door. The wall is thin.'

'Nevertheless, Monsieur, I heard nothing.'

She waltzed away, to be met at the dining-room door by the smiling, ducking head-waiter: Mimi, Madame Deslauriers, with a lot of leg showing through her slit-skirt.

We had Bavents brought into Hanson's office after I had briefed Hanson on the development. Hanson had tried to preserve his incredulity, but it was wilting under the impact of vulgar fact. He gazed indignantly as Bavents entered, still wearing his neat waiter's garb;

he didn't want Bavents, and if Bavents was chummie, Hanson was going to take it as a personal affront. Bavents barely glanced at him. He shuffled in forlornly and dropped on the chair Dutt had placed for him.

'Adam Bavents.'

He stared at me wildly.

'Please listen to me carefully. You have been charged with possession of cannabis resin, but now I am going to ask you some further questions. You don't have to answer them, but if you do your answers will be taken down in writing and may be used in evidence. Is that clear?'

His eyes rolled horribly, his hands moved in fluttery gestures.

'Please! I just w-want to get it over. I'll tell you anything you want to know.'

'But you understand the warning?'

'Oh God . . . ask me!'

'I wish to have your answer on record.'

He made a wretched gasping sound. 'Yes – I understand! And it's true – I killed those two men!'

'You're lying!' Hanson snarled, jumping up.

Bavents sobbed and clutched his hair-cocooned head.

I ordered coffee to give Bavents time to digest his moment of hysteria; also Hanson, who was raving quietly and spitting cheroot on the office linoleum. Then I took Bavents through it, beginning with straight questions about his acquaintance with Deslauriers in Chelsea, but nudging him into taking the initiative

181

when we came to the killings. Bavents answered well. Now he had let go the pressure, some of his hang-dog attitude had left him.

'Where did the knife come from?'

'I got it from the cook's box. One of my jobs is sharpening his knives.'

'How big?'

'Well, not very big. I wanted a knife that would go in my pocket.'

'Where is it now?'

'I put it back. Otherwise the chef would have missed it. I washed it, naturally.'

'Can you show me the knife?'

'Of course. It's the only one of that size.'

All straight-forward. But sometimes questions can be too easy to answer.

'Tell me what happened on Friday evening, beginning when you left the hotel.'

Bavents hesitated for several seconds, his eyes fixed on his knees.

'W-well, I was waiting in the yard. I knew what time he had to get there. When I heard the Bugatti's engine start I started mine and went after him. I left the Mini on the car park. Freddy was down there, sitting in his car. I c-came up behind him and let him have it. He just fell forward over the wheel.'

'What clothes were you wearing?'

'Clothes—?'

'Stabbing gives rise to spurts of blood.'

Bavents paled. 'I-I was wearing an old windcheater, one I keep for working on the car.'

'Where is it now?'

'I th-threw it in the river. I thought I'd b-better, with all that blood on it. And I washed the knife with that special cleaner which is supposed to take out blood-stains.'

I nodded. 'Go on.'

'Then I just left him. I went back to the Mini and drove back here.'

'Seeing nobody.'

'N-no, nobody. There wasn't a soul about anywhere.'

'Nobody coming down the track?'

He shook his head.

'No other cars on the park?'

He hesitated. 'Y-yes, I think there were some. But I was too worked up really to notice.'

I asked him some more, noticing specially the questions that brought about the stammer; then switched him quickly to the Bilney killing and his knowledge of the location of the chalet.

'Did Madame Deslauriers tell you about it?'

'No! But I heard her giving directions to Bilney.'

'How do you get there?'

'It's the b-back road to Sallowes. There's a turning off th-through a gate.'

'Could you drive me there?'

He swallowed. 'Yes. But I've only b-been there once.'

I was tempted to try him with a map, but had my reasons for not pressing him.

'Right. Describe what happened yesterday.'

'M-Mimi wanted me to drive her out there.'

'She did?'

183

He nodded in his hair. 'Only I couldn't get the time off. But I knew where she'd gone when she took the launch, and I thought it would give me a chance at Bilney. So I asked Mr Frayling for the afternoon and d–drove round to the chalet.'

'What time would that be?'

'I'm not s–sure. I'd say I got there about three-thirty. Anyway, he wasn't there, and the place was locked up. I had to break in through a b–back window.'

'Using what?'

He made a reaching gesture. 'I'd b–brought a tyre-lever with me.'

'Not, for example, a large screw-driver?'

'I – n–no! A tyre-lever.'

'A tyre-lever,' I said.

Bavents' eyes swivelled and he breathed a little faster. Then he started off again, filling in the words in jerks.

'I waited for him behind the door. I thought I'd hear his car pull up. Only he must have guessed I was there b–because he left his car down the track. Then he came in right fast, slamming the door back, so I couldn't get him as he came in. I had to ch–chase him into the bedroom. I g–got him down behind the bed.'

'Was he scared?'

Bavents' throat worked. 'I g–guess so.'

'Bilney was a criminal who knew about knives.'

'He tried to keep me off, but I g–got him all right. He went down. I f–finished him off.'

'Which made a lot of blood.'

Bavents nodded stupidly.

'What did you do with your clothes this time?'

'I-I'd remembered about Freddy, I was wearing a boiler suit. Then I threw that in the river too.'

I didn't ask him if he had washed the knife again. I felt I knew the answer to that one. I signalled to Dutt. He escorted Bavents out. There was a silence broken only by Hanson's gnashing of a cheroot.

I lit my pipe too and contributed my quota to the office atmosphere. Hanson, who had been hovering tigerishly in the background, now advanced and dumped himself on the desk.

'Look, it sounds as phoney as hell. But that dozey bastard just *must* have done it!'

'Why do you say that?'

'Because, Christ alive, he knows what only the chummie could know. He knows where the car was left, how the window was forced, that Bilney was knifed behind the bed. And he would probably have told us a whole lot more if you hadn't played soft and laid off him.'

'And knowing these things makes him chummie?'

'Yeah,' Hanson said. 'It flaming has to. Because we haven't leaked information at this end, and you're the tightest-mouthed sod I ever met.'

I grinned but shook my head. 'You were right the first time. He's phoney as hell.'

'But how in blazes can he be, when he sits there coughing up chapter and verse?'

'Simple. He's been briefed.'

'Briefed—?' Hanson's horse-teeth showed in a gape.

'By our ingenious friend, Mimi Deslauriers. He was in conference with her today.'

Hanson gurgled. 'But for crying aloud. You're not saying he would turn himself in for Mimi?'

'Why not?'

'Why not? What good will it do him if he ends up sitting out a lifer?'

'He won't.' I feathered smoke. 'I'm sure that's not the plot at all. Once Bavents has served his turn we shall find he has alibis a yard long. Mimi can clear him of the Quarles killing whenever her memory starts to improve, and there will be fireproof witnesses around somewhere to place him in Norchester yesterday afternoon. All Bavents is risking is a charge of obstruction, for which he'll probably get off with a wigging. And the possession charge is a first offence. You can guess who'll be picking up the fine.'

'But for Christ-sake, why?'

'Mimi wants the heat off. Our camping on her doorstep is cramping her style.'

'Like a bear's backside!' Hanson snarled. 'From now on she'll only draw breath when we do.'

I gentled smoke at him. 'No.'

'You aim to let her get away with it?'

'Mimi has made her first mistake. Bavents wasn't up to the job of conning us.'

'So we give her three cheers?'

'What she has let out is that she's in touch with the real killer. Before, we suspected it. Now we know it. We are going to play the game from there.'

'Like pulling her in!'

'Not like that. She doesn't know we've seen through Bavents.'

Hanson spat cheroot. 'Fine. But I can't see a sweat-session doing any harm.'

I aimed more smoke at him. 'What we're going to do is withdraw the police presence from Haughton. Bavents can go up on the possession charge, and you'll see the beak and get a remand. There mustn't be as much as a traffic cop at Haughton. Mimi will be free to go or stay. Free to meet or contact whom she pleases. Nobody will bother her at all.'

Hanson traded smoke for smoke. 'And meanwhile you'll go chase your tail?'

I shook my head. 'I'll be sitting on it. But on the outside, looking in.'

CHAPTER EIGHTEEN

I GAVE HER the key of the Bugatti the next morning, in what turned out to be a touching ceremony. It took place after breakfast, in the hall, where Dutt's bag and mine were already waiting. Mimi dropped a tear and pressed the key to her bosom. The gesture was so natural that one could almost believe it. Then she stood by sadly, the key in her hand, while I wrote out a chit for Frayling.

'Of course, my friend, I understand what this means. The poor yak didn't serve at table this morning. And now you are leaving. It is a melancholy moment. I wish I could think that you were wrong.'

I bowed my regrets.

'Are you so certain?'

'I'm afraid I mustn't discuss the matter.'

She nodded. 'But you have given me the key. You would not do that if there were still doubts.' She eyed me earnestly. 'Is that not so?'

'You must draw your own conclusions, Madame. We shall probably need your testimony later. But just now we have no further business with you.'

She sighed. 'Yet I wish I could help him.'

'I don't think you should waste your sympathy.'

She sighed at this, too. 'Yet it is so sad. My only consolation is to have met you, Monsieur.'

I should have kissed her hand, but anyway she waved it as Dutt and I drove off in the Lotus. When I saw in the rear-view mirror that she had gone back into the hotel, I made a left turn and drove round the block. Hanson was waiting at the rear of the bank. He had brought an unmarked Capri, which he had borrowed from Traffic. I parked the Lotus, leaving the engine running, and Hanson slipped me the key of the Capri. 'Everything fixed?'

'Roger. Now I'm off back to process Bavents.'

'Watch the Lotus. It can go to your head.'

Hanson grunted, got in and gunned away.

We entered the bank by a service door and were met inside by the manager. He introduced us to his head cashier, who was the tenant of the flat above. Hanson had done all the explaining. The cashier led us up outside steps. We were admitted to the flat by his wife, a snub-nosed woman with ginger hair.

'Come this way, sir.'

She showed us into a bedroom furnished with a pleasant-looking teak suite. Venetian blinds were dropped over the two windows, before each of which had been placed a chair. I went to the nearest one. The blind-slats were slanted to give a view across and below; I found myself staring at the blue Bugatti and, behind it, Frayling, sitting in his office.

'Is this how you want it, sir?'

'Exactly right. Have you any objection to our smoking?

She smiled. 'No, sir. We're both of us smokers.'

She brought us ash-trays. And we sat.

It was a number of years since I had been on a stake-out, and my ennui-index had risen in the interval. To a certain extent I had lost the faculty of watching while allowing my mind to pursue its courses. Not much was happening down there below. I soon tired of trying to memorize the traffic. The shadow of the bank, tucked in beneath us, seemed never to shorten as the minutes limped by. Three guests fetched their cars, four set out on foot; a butcher, a baker, a green-grocer delivered. Two guests returned, one carrying a parcel. Frayling appeared and disappeared in his office. Out of sight in the kitchen, minus Bavents, they would be busy preparing food for lunch, while maids were hoovering in the bedrooms and barmen washing and stacking glasses. But Mimi? The only token of Mimi was the Bugatti basking in the sun. Was it possible she had left it there for me to gaze at, while she slipped away in a launch?

'Sir!'

Dutt was poking towards his slats; Mimi had appeared, and I had nearly missed her. She was seated in the office in her usual style, her feet up, the phone in her hand. She was laughing, trilling strings of words; in her other hand a cigarette. Relaxed, unhurried; filling in the small-talk; somebody she liked: somebody she loved.

'What do you make of that, sir?'

Mimi had hung up and taken some dancing steps from the office.

'It could have been lover boy.'

'It looked like the green light, sir.'

'So let us hope there is nothing holding him back.'

Time, eleven-twenty-one. I tried to think of some circumstance suggested by the time for lover boy's availability. I failed, but it didn't bother me: didn't spoil the picture of Mimi's sweet confidence.

'I'd say it was a local call, sir. I was watching her dial. Don't think it was more than six figures.'

'She might have been gassing to a girl-friend.'

'Not that one, sir. She doesn't go in for them.'

We settled again, with renewed alertness. But that was the high spot of the morning. The next excitement was opening time with its quick build-up of male custom. Some of the patrons were familiar to us, regulars from nearby shops and offices; but there was a healthy residuum of casuals, holiday-makers and visiting businessmen. We tried to filter them. Reps you could identify fairly easily by their cars. Older men were probably out, also men of poor physique and provincial style. What emerged were three possibles, young men with looks, bodies and arguable panache. One arrived on foot, one was driving a Fiat, and one a much-accessoried M.G. Each of them stopped to admire the Bugatti but they were not alone in this; as a custom-maker a Bugatti would be worth its weight to any brewery.

'Any preferences?' I asked Dutt.

'I like the bloke who walked in, sir. I don't think chummie would just drive up here. He would want to prowl around first.'

'Did you think the Fiat-driver looked familiar?'

'Bit of the pop-singer about him, sir. Maybe we've seen him on the telly.'

'Maybe,' I said. 'Speak for yourself.'

In the event the Fiat-driver had stopped only for a quick one; while the pedestrian, who soon followed him out, was claimed by a girl driving a Volks. The M.G.-decorator was the stayer; he had probably decided to wait for lunch. He was lowest on the list: no vulnerable chummie would have given much time to a comic M.G.

'Excuse me, sir.'

It was the cashier's wife, who had come in with a tray of beer and sandwiches. She was smiling embarrassedly: because, after all, she was entertaining two strange men in her bedroom.

'Nobody said anything about your meals . . .'

They were hefty sandwiches of ham and tomato. I made her an offer of a subsistence payment, which only embarrassed her the more.

'No, we are happy to help the police – my husband being what he is.'

'But we pay for our rations.'

'No – please! We would like to do our bit to help.'

Strange attitude from a member of the public. We ate her sandwiches and drank her beer. At two-forty the M.G.-driver claimed his car and drove off alone.

We waited some more.

Now the sun had worked round to our side of the flat and the Bugatti was inching its way into shade. The bedroom was muggy. We couldn't open the windows without raising the blinds, which we daren't risk. The scene below had fallen asleep; no traffic passed for minutes at a time. Frayling visited his office at ten minutes past three, but then was absent for two long hours. Entertainment unlimited; my pipe tasted vile and the beer and close atmosphere made me feel torpid. I kept awake mainly by debating with myself whether it was I or Mimi who was being the smart one.

Dutt, too, was doing his policeman's fret.

'Do you think we should have started at the other end, sir?'

'Dainty is on the job. I rang him last night. Any information will come straight here.'

'Has he any ideas?'

'Just Whitey Ferrier.'

Dutt sniffed. 'Whitey wouldn't do the job himself.'

'So we're watching for who did.'

Dutt pulled out a sigh. 'It would still be nice to know who we're expecting.'

He didn't add, or if he is coming: which was what the conversation was really about.

At four-thirty two guests returned, breaking a dead-spell of fifty minutes. The shadow on the Bugatti had reached the cockpit-cover, which I had buttoned-on last evening. A newsboy pushed his bike along the pavement and stopped to make a delivery at the Barge-House; Fritz, the German waiter, ran after him and returned with a copy of a sporting paper. Life beginning again. By five, an intermittent stream of traffic had developed. Five-ten, Frayling reappeared to talk patiently and lengthily into the telephone.

Five-twenty, two more returning guests. Five-thirty, a sudden explosion of giggling shop-girls. It had been a rough afternoon, but the swinging evening was at hand.

'Excuse me, sir.'

Our embarrassed lady was back again with tea and cake. We munched and drank, keeping only half an eye on the glaring slats and the view between them. Were we making fools of ourselves? It had begun to seem like it, after a solid eight hours of sitting and watching. Trying to feel like cops on a job while the working world went on around us. Mimi hadn't been bluffed. I had taken the bait too easily, hadn't probed and questioned in the way she had expected. She had borrowed the office, rung her man, but hadn't signalled him to come running. Non, Monsieur, non. Why had I thought it would be so simple?

'Car pulling on to the apron, sir.'

I swallowed cake and took a look. The car was a commonplace green 1100, rather dusty, with a J registration. A man got out. He was something of an eyeful, dressed in the full boutique gear: a draping floral shirt-jacket over matching bell-bottom trousers, with suede boots. He had shoulder-length black hair and wore baroque sun-glasses.

'Chelsea, here I come,' Dutt murmured.

'Know him?'

'No, sir. But he looks a good spec. I could see him stepping out with the lady.'

We watched. He paused beside the Bugatti. I judged his height at five-eleven; strongly-built, with good shoulders; handsome features, lightly tanned.

He glanced around him with quick alertness, then un-buttoned one corner of the Bugatti's cover. He stared inside, at the dials, the controls; then re-buttoned the cover and went into the Barge-House.

'A bit of a cheeky chummie, sir.'

I shrugged. 'I think I would have done the same myself. But the 1100 does have a London area regis-tration. There'll be no harm in giving it a check.'

Dutt slipped out to use the cashier's phone. I drank tea with my eye on the Barge-House. Lucky after all? Or was this one more holiday-maker, ordering dinner, waiting for opening time? The clothes didn't match what I was expecting, but the clothes could be a clever disguise; nobody would expect a fugitive killer to dress like a Carnaby Street peacock. And there would be Mimi's brain behind that one: Mimi, who didn't miss a trick. So why not? What would look more natural than Chelsea Joe turning up at the Barge-House?

Dutt came back. 'It's pinched, sir. On the Met list for last Friday.'

'Friday?'

'Yes, sir. Some time in the P.M. From Norland Road, off Holland Park.'

The district meant nothing. Dutt's eye had a gleam in it.

'We could go down there and nab him, sir.'

'For what?' I said. 'Stealing a car? That's all we have on him at the moment.'

'It would make a start, sir.'

I shook my head. 'I think we'll wait a little longer. Just to see if Mimi will tip us her hand. When she does will be the time to move.'

We stood now at the one window, waiting, willing events to happen. But once more time began to build up, minute laying itself to minute. The bar had opened, a little cluster of custom had formed from leaving-off shop and office staff. The commuter traffic had passed its peak and pedestrians stood chatting on the pavement. Behind us we could hear a faint clinking of dishes as the cashier and his wife ate their evening meal, along with the low monotone of the television rounding up the regional news. The day relaxing. And now the Bugatti was sitting full in the advancing shade.

Then Frayling backed into view in the office, a slip of paper in his hand. A cheque: and he was chatting animatedly to someone as he unlocked a drawer of the desk and took out a cash-box. He nodded and smiled and nodded again before turning his attention to the cash-box. A few moments later the swing-door opened: and out stepped Mimi and Chelsea Joe.

He was carrying her luggage: two neat, jazzy suitcases and a coat of featherweight blue mink. Mimi was laughing. She was wearing a dusty pink two-piece, the least casual garb I had seen her in yet. They went to the Bugatti. He stripped off the cover, tilted forward the seats and loaded the suitcases. Then he held the coat for Mimi to slip into, a proceeding which she delayed by giving him a kiss.

'Let's go!' Dutt muttered.

'Wait.'

Now Chelsea Joe had gone to the 1100. He unlocked the boot and took from it a canvas holdall and a black suitcase. The suitcase fitted in with Mimi's cases, but the holdall was too bulky. He took a spider from the Bugatti's luggage-hold and secured the holdall to the car's small grid.

'Right.'

We hustled out of the bedroom and down the outside stairs to the Capri. I started the engine, drifted the Capri forward, and halted it, still in the cover of the bank.

'Report in.'

'Shouldn't we grab him now, sir?'

'I want to see which way they are heading.'

Reluctantly Dutt picked up the transceiver and made contact with HQ. I waited, listening. The roll of the Bugatti's engine broke in suddenly on the Capri's murmur. Chelsea Joe gunned it three or four times, then I could hear it shifting in the direction of the junction. I sneaked the Capri out. The Bugatti was turning right towards the bridge and Norchester. I let a couple of cars go by, eased the Capri on to the Bugatti's tail.

'They're off back to town, sir.'

'We shall see.'

We trailed the Bugatti through Wrackstead. But beyond the village his winker went and he turned left into the road to Sallowes. This lost me my cover. I lingered on the turn, letting him go another hundred yards up. He wasn't racing. I had the impression that the Bugatti was as novel to him as it had been to me.

'They wouldn't be heading for the chalet, sir?'

'Report his direction.'

'Yes, sir. The patrols are converging.'

'No contact yet. Tell them to stay clear.'

Dutt spoke his piece and was grittily answered.

Not the chalet. The Bugatti passed that turning and rumbled on into Sallowes village. There it hesitated at a cross-roads, and eventually turned left. The signpost said: Ockley.

'Check with the map.'

Dutt took a map from the glove-locker. The road we had joined was some sort of B road, but it was tracking purposefully across the open country. There were fast stretches, tempting Chelsea Joe to get the feel of a vintage sixty. My nose said we were pointing eastwards, and a church across the fields offered confirmation.

'About six to Ockley, sir.'

'Then?'

'Ockley is on the main Norchester-Starmouth road. So he could go either way there, except it would be a roundabout way to Norchester.'

'But it would be the direct way to Starmouth.'

'Yes, sir. Couldn't be more direct.'

'What's marked at Starmouth?'

Dutt peered at the map. 'There's an airfield and a roll-on, roll-off ferry to Rotterdam.'

'A ferry!'

'Yes, sir.'

'Buzz control. We'll have the patrols pick him up now.'

I closed on the Bugatti, which was whipping along at plus-sixty. I could perhaps have taken him, perhaps not: anyway, I decided not to try. Heroic measures make good film but tend to prejudice public safety.

I needed only to keep my eye on him. The patrols would do the rest.

We reached Ockley, where Chelsea Joe had to halt at the main road junction. I looked round for the patrol cars, but apparently we had got there first. Joe surged off again; then, as I followed him, caught sight of the Capri in his mirror. Mimi's scarfed head jerked round: her big eyes stared at me. Directly, the Bugatti began drawing away.

I cursed to myself and squeezed the Capri. I knew the stretch from Ockley to Starmouth. Dead level, it stretched across the marshes with only one bend in ten miles. The Bugatti could lose me by sheer horse-power if Chelsea Joe kept it booming. And there was a side-road, just one, where the main road made its bend.

'Report in.'

We came out of the village trailing the Bugatti by a hundred yards. It doubled that distance in the next half-mile down the flat, pollard-willow-lined straight.

'Two patrols heading this way from Starmouth, sir.'

'Tell them to switch on lights and sirens.'

The Capri was revving its sophisticated heart out and still the Bugatti was growing smaller. It reached an almost-level bridge, where a dyke passed under: I saw daylight briefly beneath its four wheels. We hit the bridge and skipped too, and probably landed a lot lighter. But it made no odds: we were being dis-tanced; Ettore was having the last laugh. Quarter of a mile had stretched into a half, and soon the half would be three-quarters.

'Lights over there, sir.'

Away across the marsh were a pair of faintly sparking roof-lights. They were hurrying along on a diagonal towards the dog-leg bend, about a mile ahead.

'What do you think they will do, sir?'

'Get them a message. If chummie sees them he'll take the side-road.'

'He's probably spotted them already, sir.'

'Tell them just to haul up and make a block.'

I lost sight of them. Perhaps they had switched off their lights. But half a minute later it was academic. I saw Chelsea Joe's brake-lights glow at the bend. Then he crossed the verge and hit a tree.

We screamed in from one direction and the patrol cars from the other. The Bugatti had bounced clear of the tree and slipped nose-down into a dyke. Chelsea Joe was still with it; he was flaked out over the big wheel. Mimi had landed in a thicket of bush-willow, from which, amazingly, she was beginning to crawl. She was nearest to the patrols, so we left her to them and went down to rescue Chelsea Joe.

He had got a cut forehead, which was bleeding prettily, but a quick check revealed no broken bones. He was out cold. We lifted him up the dyke-bank and stretched him gingerly on the verge. I felt a twinge of recognition as I stared down at the blood-smeared features: the good-looking lines of the nose and cheekbones, the primitive chin and the loose-lipped mouth. Dutt knelt to dab the gashed forehead, then gave a startled exclamation.

'This is a wig, sir!'

He grabbed the black locks: they came away in his hand. Underneath was pale, golden-brown hair, cut medium-length, and short side-boards. Now I knew who he was.

'Would you call that hair fair?'

Dutt gazed incredulously. 'Holy Jesus! Could this be the original Peter Robinson?'

'I think it could. And the driver of the Viva. Which is why we found it wiped clean.'

'So Bilney was a con!'

'Bilney was a mug. There's not much doubt what brought him up here.'

I scrambled back down the bank to the tilted Bugatti and salvaged the black suitcase from the luggage-hold. It was locked, but there were tools handy and I burst the catches with a screwdriver. The suitcase was stuffed with bank-notes. Most of them were still in wrappers. Some were spotted with dark stains and stains had been scrubbed from the lining of the lid. I slammed the lid shut and returned to Dutt.

'It's all there in one parcel. And chummie's tan is a home-grown product.'

Dutt nodded dully.

'It's Fring.'

A sharp cry behind us made us turn: Mimi was standing there between two patrolmen. Her eyes were fixed fascinatedly on Fring, who still lay senseless and lazily bleeding. She made a sudden move forward, but I got in front of her.

'No. It is best that you don't see him.'

'But I must go to him!'

'No. There is nothing you can do for him now.'

I drew her away to one of the patrol-cars. She wailed touchingly, but didn't resist. Her Balmain suit was rent and muddy, but otherwise she appeared in fair fettle. I sat her in the rear of the car, which faced away from the crash, and went round to take a seat beside her.

'Now, Madame Deslauriers, I need some answers. Fring's troubles are settled, yours are just beginning.'

'Oh Monsieur, you are heartless!'

'The first question is this. Do I charge you as accessory to one or both killings?'

'I, Monsieur!' She jerked indignantly upright. 'But I had nothing to do with either of them.'

'It's your choice,' I shrugged. 'But you had better explain. Because only you can help yourself now.'

Mimi, Madame Deslauriers, glared at me. 'This is altogether too much! I am the person to whom all this is happening, and now you tell me that I am to blame?'

'You sent Fring after Freddy.'

'Oh, it isn't true! Did I know that Jimmy was going to kill him?'

'Didn't you?'

'No! I thought he would beat him up. Are you telling me now that Freddy didn't deserve it?'

'Was it Freddy who shopped them?'

'Who else? It was how he planned to get rid of Jimmy. He couldn't bear me loving Jimmy better than him. He wished to get rid of him, to close up business. And all that he boasted to me after the hold-up.

Is it any wonder I helped Jimmy? But not if I knew he was going to kill him, oh no! You cannot blame me for that.'

'Yet it didn't seem to trouble you.'

'What could I do? You would not expect me to shop Jimmy.'

'And the second killing?'

'Oh, Monsieur! Who asked the stupid Bilney to steal money? He was a burglar, a common thief. It was no matter what happened to him.'

'So Fring caught him at it.'

'Just so. He had found the money under the floor-board. He had his dirty fingers in it when Jimmy went in there. That is all there is about that.'

'Which Fring explained when you phoned him.'

'Yes, I rang to warn him about you.'

'And you told him to get out, and to take Bilney's car.'

'Was it not right I should help to think for him?' She sniffed feelingly. 'And it was all going well. He had even succeeded in buying a passport. Oh, Monsieur, it is desolating. This is not how such a boy should have died.'

'Look in the mirror,' I said.

She stared at me suspiciously before craning her head to look. What she saw was James Fring being helped into an ambulance by SJAB men. Mimi exploded. I took a fist in the mouth, then she kicked me and went for the door. No use: I'd bolted the child-lock. Mimi roared at the top of her lungs.

'Pig! Pig! Pig!'

'Cool down,' I said. 'We'll convict him anyway.'

'You have tricked me. Oh, I hate you! I wish that you were dead too.'

'But you are going to give me a statement.'

'No — never!'

I nodded. 'Yes, I think you will. You being such a sensible, logical Frenchwoman. And after all, you're not very much in love with Fring.'

She spoke rapid, idiomatic French.

'Listen,' I said. 'This is why you will. I am going to charge you in any case, but if you give me the statement the charge will be accessory after the fact. That is not so serious, and with a clever counsel you will probably get off with a suspended sentence. But if I have to charge you as an accessory before and after the fact, then you will be in the same boat as Fring. That will mean a life-sentence. You will be over forty when they let you out of Holloway.'

'I tell you, never!'

'Think about it, Mimi. Make your gesture but pull the chain.'

She spat at me, but missed. We sat gazing into each other's eyes.

Rigby House, Norwich,
November 1971–March 1972